LEAN BUT
NOT MEAN

Alex Duran

LEAN BUT
NOT MEAN

Table of Contents

Acknowledgments

I would like to honor and dedicate this book to my mother Alice Nieves who left us last year, and my 3 year old daughter Lexington. Who brings a life of happiness and continue to be an inspiration for getting ahead in life. I appreciate everything God has given me in a family and life.

I would like to pay tribute to the thousands of children who have been a part of Fitwize 4 Kids and changed their lives through our nutrition and fitness programs. May they continue their journey toward a healthy lifestyle through adulthood. Fitwize 4 Kids will continue helping to fight childhood inactivity and obesity, and to provide an environment where kids feel safe, have fun, and learn how to live a healthy lifestyle!

www.fitwize4kids.com

A QUICK GLIMPSE OF THE AUTHOR'S PAST

Growing up in New York City, I had my own personal bullies. One went by the name of Ozmel, and he was the biggest kid in my neighbourhood and school. Every morning Ozmel's fist was always finding its way to my head each time I rode the bus to school, and no one ever helped me all through three grades. The most shocking moment was when he tied me to a pole while he tried to put firecrackers in my mouth and then try to light them up.

My two other bullies – you're not going to believe – were twin brothers called Bruce and Lee. YES! They made it hard, day after day, to go to school. Bruce and Lee beat me up the same time every time every week on Friday like clockwork. My mom one day made me stand up and fight both of them at the same time, and I got beat up pretty badly; my mom regrets it to this day.

At home, food was not our friend. I remember one time my mom and I went to a fast food place for dinner, and she super sized her meal before super size was even on the market. Not to mention, we would go and buy clothes, and there wasn't a whole lot she and my sister could wear. The mirror was not their friend. They were always embarrassed or depressed about the way they looked. As a result, my sister was constantly picked on at school.

There are many kids out there who have no help against being overweight or being bullied. Too often, kids are not getting attention or even noticed until the moment something goes really wrong and it's too late. It takes something drastic and dramatic for something to change.

Chapter One

Red Alert

Jonny Fatzio slowed his pace as he headed towards the north corner of Woodside Junior High. He squinted as he looked across the ball diamond. All clear. He glanced back over his shoulder. A large group of students bunched up near the buses. They weren't going to cause him any hassle.

Jonny slowed to a stop as he reached the corner. Here the solid brick wall of the school came to an end. Beyond it lay open territory, enemy occupied. Jonny's sneakers scuffled in the dust. His heart pounded. Licking his dry lips, he scanned the expanse of grass. It seemed miles to the far fence line with its gate onto the sidewalk and the city street. Why did the school yard have to be so huge? It was like a prairie out there! Could he make it across to the gate without being seen?

Go, get going now! his mind yelled at him.

Maybe his enemies were in detention, just for a

change. Maybe he was going to have a relaxing stroll home. Yeah, right. With one last glance towards the gate, Jonny stepped away from the wall of the school and headed onto the empty grass.

"Securing the perimeters?" drawled a sarcastic voice.

Steve the Peeve!

Johnny's head jerked, muscles clenched. His eyes darted right and left. He was just in time to spot the three members of Steve's gang step into the sunshine. Dang! They'd been hiding behind a blue metal dumpster. It must have been put there for the construction company that was renovating the Shop classroom.

Hunching his shoulders, Jonny fought down the urge to run. Stay cool, he warned himself. Just walk. But his legs seemed to pick up speed on their own, galloping along. Johnny's round, lumpy shadow surged over the grass. His sticky thighs rubbed together.

"Runs good for a hippo, doesn't he?" shouted Pete the Cheat.

Liz, the only girl in the gang, gave a high pitched giggle. Her laughter was worse than fingernails on a blackboard! "Hey, Jelly Fatso, what's your rush?" she screamed.

Jonny gave up listening to that voice in his head that was repeating, Stay cool. Panicked, he rushed across the grass, headed for the gate onto the street. If he could just get there, maybe he could sort of merge with other people going by. Even that old lady who sometimes walked a bunch of yappy dogs might offer a tiny bit of protection.

Johnny's lungs burned and his ribs heaved. He was panting now like a dog himself. Behind, he could hear the swift, light footsteps of the gang as they chased him.

Suddenly he tripped. Flying through the air headfirst, he saw grass rushing to meet him. His stomach slammed into ground hard as concrete after a dry summer. Breath whooshed from Johnny's lungs. He gasped, helpless, dark spots swirling in his head. His heart and the feet of the gang thundered in unison.

A toe nudged the rolls along his ribs.

"Thought he woulda bounced, being so round and all." Steve's mocking voice rang in Jonny's ears. Jonny covered his head with his hands, waiting for a harder kick.

"Hey, Jelly Fatso," said Pete, "how much chicken food does your mom give you?"

Jonny moaned and gripped his head tighter. Through one eye he could see the toes of Steve's black army surplus boots. He knew, from past contact with them, they had steel toes.

A boot toe nudged closer to Johnny's elbow, jammed into the prickly grass. "Answer Pete's question!" Steve said arrogantly.

"Wha- what? I can't remember the question!" Jonny said.

"How much chicken feed does it take to make you such a fat chicken?" Pete asked.

Jonny groaned again. There was no good answer, nothing he could say that would get him out of trouble.

He opened one eye again, searching for Steve's steel toe. It seemed to have moved. Not a good sign. He might be swinging back for a kick. Liz's ankle, with its tattoo of a black rose, moved past Johnny's face. She should've just had a thorn put there, Jonny thought, not for the first time. It was hard to believe he'd been friends with her in grades one and two.

His mind blanked out as he glimpsed the swing of Steve's boot. He rolled over, away from it. The toe caught him on the left shoulder. A holler of pain escaped from his mouth.

He tensed for another blow. Suddenly, panting and yipping seeped into his ears. "What's wrong over there?" called a thin voice. "Is the boy hurt? Do you need help?"

What now? Jonny wondered. He rolled further away as Steve, Pete, and Liz stepped back. Across the grass rushed a fluffy dust storm of little dogs. Their pink tongues flapped. They strained at their leashes, somehow not getting tangled up, and dragged along a wispy woman.

She peered down at Jonny. "Are you hurt?" she asked again.

"No, ma'am," he said. "I just – I just –"

"He tripped over his shoe laces. See, one is untied," Liz said in a sweet tone. "Let me tie it up for you, Jonny."

Liz kneeled in the grass, but Jonny yanked his

foot back. "I can tie my own laces," he muttered. He heaved himself into a sitting position. The fluffy dogs leaped against his chest, grinning and panting. They licked his chubby fingers as he struggled to knot the trailing lace of one sneaker. He tied them extra tight, humiliated that it had slipped undone and sent him crashing to the ground. In front of the gang! Was he cursed or what?

Steve, Liz, and Pete turned and drifted away over the field. Pete, skinny as a popsicle stick and always a follower, stuck his hands deep into his pockets. He was copying Steve, trying for the same relaxed swagger. But only Steve had steel toes instead of sneakers. Only Steve belonged to a boxing club and could beat the daylights out of anyone. Especially a fat kid.

"Are they friends of yours?" The scrawny lady was staring down at Jonny. Her eyes behind large rounded glasses were bright blue. Thick mascara coated her lashes. Wasn't that a little strange in someone so old? She had to be at least seventy if she was a day.

Jonny shrugged. "They're just kids from my class," he muttered. He struggled to his feet while the little dogs jumped around. Jonny bent to pet their fluffy heads.

If only I could hang out with dogs instead of kids, he thought. But he'd given up asking for a dog. Dad worked long hours in the city center, doing who knew what with things called stock options on the 28th floor of a glass tower. And Mom rushed in and out at home, cheery, yakking on her cell phone. She was a top-selling realtor. Jonny knew phrases like desirable neighborhood and rezoning application before he even started kindergarten. No, Mom and Dad had explained over and over that they were too busy to add a dog to the family. Even though dogs were almost the only things that made Johnny's chest loosen up against tension. Role-playing video games worked fine too, sucking him away into other worlds. There he could wield a sword and be a hero.

"Well, I'd better get these little rascals back to their dinners," the old lady said. "You get on home now, boy." She shot Jonny a bright stare as if she knew how his legs felt weak as hotdog buns. Then she hauled the dogs around until they were all facing the fence. In a moment, they were bouncing across the grass, yapping and barking. They hauled the old lady through the gate onto the sidewalk and out of sight.

Jonny followed slowly. Today, he'd get safely home, but that still left tomorrow to face them, and the day after…all the days from now until next year when he finished grade seven. He didn't think he could face so many days of terror. He might just die from accumulated fright. It would build up in his system, bloating his body until one day his skin turned green and he keeled over, right in the middle of class…

Trudging along, he barely noticed the swish of passing cars. Trees cast shade over his head. The odd stray leaf drifted down, getting ready for a Halloween extravaganza. People passed by: a jogger, a mom pushing a stroller, an old man with a newspaper under one arm.

It was only four blocks of residential homes from Woodside Junior High to Jonny's house. As he reached the last intersection before home, he caught a glimpse of brilliant tropical colors up ahead. His heart sank like a stone. Was it her? Could it really be? He stopped and stared.

Yep, it was her, all right: that new girl who'd started school yesterday. Brenda Sloten, she was called. Yesterday she'd worn neon pink jeggings and a shirt with crazy swirls. Today, her bulky body was covered in flowered ruffles, orange and hot pink again. And today's jeggings were orange too. Like a really big Hawaiian sunset, Jonny thought. But what's she doing here?

Jonny slipped into the shadow of some shrubbery and watched. Brenda turned into his own street! Jonny's heart sank lower. She strolled along, past Johnny's pale blue ranch house, past the neighbor's. Her figure dwindled from view as she reached the next intersection and turned right. Right into Carambola Circle, a dead-end street!

Which means, she's gotta walk past my house every single day to get to school, Jonny thought. If the gang see Brenda and me walking along together, they'll massacre us. We'd look like a small herd of buffalo!

If only his best friend, Jason, hadn't moved away last year. He and Jason had always walked to school together. It was after Jason moved that the bullying really began.

Now, Jonny waited until Brenda disappeared up the circle. Then he made a dash for his own front door. His backpack dragged on his shoulders, heavy with homework stuff. Jonny wasn't sure it would make it through the school year. He wasn't sure he'd make it through the year – or even until Christmas. First the gang to avoid, and now the fat new girl to avoid. He really was cursed.

Chapter Two

Who's The Boss?

Jonny climbed the six brick-stoned steps to his front door. His mother's flowers that she called foundation plantings were withering up now summer was over.

Jonny fumbled in his backpack and pulled out his front door key. A knot of tension slipped loose in his chest. In another moment, he'd be safe inside. But then there'd be new problems to deal with.

"Do. Not. Lose. This!" his father had said, handing Jonny the key the night before school started.

"I won't," Jonny had promised. His parents had been discussing after-school arrangements all summer.

"He's old enough now to be home by himself for a couple of hours each day," Jonny's father had said.

"Are you comfortable with this, honey?" his mother had asked.

She'd seemed so concerned that Jonny

immediately straightened his shoulders and said loudly, "I'm fine, quit fussing about it."

But now that the school year had begun, he wasn't so sure that he was fine. For starters, he was terrified of losing the key. What if Pete the Cheat stole it from his pack? In grade five, Jonny had heard a story about some kids who'd climbed in the basement window of some other kid's house. They'd poured milk all over the carpets and stuck chewing gum on the furniture. Rumor was, the leader of those vandals had been Steve the Peeve. And everyone knew that Pete the Cheat had stolen people's homework and handed it in as his own to get a passing grade. So what if he stole Jonny's key, and then the gang walked straight in the front door without bothering about basement windows, and made a mess of Mom's beige furniture?

There was another problem. When Jonny let himself in with his own key, the house seemed to grow. It was like something out of that dorky Alice in Wonderland book. It stretched and grew around Jonny until it was enormous. The entrance lobby was like a giant cave coated in pale paint the color of mushrooms. The hallway to the kitchen stretched away like a funfair tunnel.

Finally, there was the silence. As soon as Jonny swung the front door closed, the silence in the house opened up like a shark's mouth and swallowed him alive. It had never done that when he and Jason came home together. All through grades one to five, he and Jason spent the after-school hours with a sitter named

Sammie. Jason's parents and his own parents split the cost of Sammie's pay. Last year, Sammie went off to college. The parents decided that, now Jonny and Jason were in grade six, they could be home without a sitter for a couple of hours. Sometimes they hung out at Jonny's place. Other days, they chilled at Jason's house further along the street. Either way, it was all good. They played video games and watched shows. They traded each other stuff like baseball cards, gaming magazines, and bags of cheese balls.

Now, a young couple with no kids lived in Jason's house, and Jonny came home alone. But he was developing survival skills.

First rule: Drop homework books with a thud and kick off sneakers.

Second rule: Rush to kitchen as fast as possible and open the fridge and check in the cupboard where Mom kept snacks.

Third rule: Turn on a video game.

Today, Jonny found that Mom had restocked the snack cupboard earlier in the day, while he was at school. Perhaps she'd had time to go shopping in between touring clients through houses for sale.

"Awesome!" he said, pulling out a bag of spicy chips. He grabbed two cans of soda to wash the chips down and cool his sizzling tongue. He started towards the family room, but then he thought maybe he should grab something sweet to round out his snack. He went back to the kitchen and took a handful of wafer cookies from the cupboard.

In the family room, he arranged his food along one arm of the black leather sofa. The silence was starting to really bug him now, swimming right up behind him and making hairs stand up on the back of his neck. He grabbed the remote controller for his X-Box and hit the power button. Once he had the screen lit up and the volume cranked, he stuffed chips into his mouth. The house seemed to shrink back to a more normal size. The sharky silence swam back out to sulk in the hall closet. Best of all, he totally forgot about Pete, Steve, and Liz.

Jonny got down to the serious business of beating a level. First he needed to win a couple of other weapons and a cloak of invisibility. His thumbs flew over the controller, his sword slashing up from the bottom of the widescreen TV mounted on the wall. Sometimes he was so busy fighting that he almost forgot to eat. But not for long.

He took a break when he beat the level and finished up the wafer cookies. They tasted sort of pink and fake, like candyfloss. Jonny smiled. When Maria got that stuff stuck in her hair last year, was Mom freaked! he remembered. Mom had whisked Maria off to a hair salon, and Jonny's little sister had her long waving curls cut off. It was the only way to get rid of the candyfloss. Maria came home with short hair. It took Jonny awhile to get used to her looking so different. She reminded him of a chubby Italian statue, like the ones in the gardens of fancy homes Mom sold.

Jonny chased a few crumbs off his lips with his

tongue. The digital wall clock said it was almost five pm. Another hour until Dad brings Maria home from her after-school program, Jonny thought. He wondered what time Mom would come in and whether she'd bring some take-out food home or whether they'd all drive into town for a restaurant meal. Maybe they could go to that Thai place that he liked, and he could order spicy chicken with lemon grass. Or maybe Mom wouldn't even make it home for dinner tonight, and Dad would take Jonny and Maria to the burger place five blocks south, in the strip mall. Either way, Jonny figured it might be a while before he got dinner. He padded back into the kitchen and opened a bag of cheese puffs.

I should be doing my homework, he thought. But I gotta beat another level to get my cloak of invisibility.

If only he could get one of these for school! He could slide right on by the gang and they wouldn't even know they were missing a chance to use the swords of their tongues against him. They wouldn't even be able to see the droop of his pants hanging beneath the swell of his belly. They wouldn't be able to place bets on how many pounds he'd gained over the summer holidays when he'd pretty much sat on the couch snacking for an entire two months.

Even in the video game, getting the invisibility cloak was difficult. But at least in the game, Jonny had other weapons. For one thing, he had a wolf that could use its super sense of smell to find enemies before they could attack. The wolf was called Shadow. For another thing, Jonny was role playing as a warrior-magician. He had totally awesome magic skills and could whip up any magic potion that was needed. It was like being in chemistry class at school, mixing stuff together to make other stuff happen. Chemistry was Johnny's favorite class and last year, he'd gotten a straight A for it.

Once, in chemistry class, tattooed Liz had put her hand up. When the teacher nodded in her direction, Liz said in a whiney tone," I don't see why we have to learn all this stuff. It's useless in real life."

"I'm sorry you find it boring," the teacher replied. "But it's not useless in real life. Chemistry is happening every time you cook something delicious, mixing and changing all your fresh ingredients into a tasty meal."

Liz rolled her eyes when the teacher turned her back. "Cooking is totally freaking boring too," she muttered to the kid seated next to her.

"I'll see you in detention after school," the teacher said, just like that, without even turning around.

For once in his life, Jonny got to smirk at Liz because he was an A student and she was failing the class. But he paid for his smirk later when the gang chased him almost all the way home, and he nearly ran smack into a skateboarder. "Whoa, dude, take a chill pill!" the boarder yelled at him. Now that would have been a good time to have an invisibility cloak.

Jonny was still trying to get the video game's cloak an hour later when car doors slammed in the driveway. Soon the door opened, and Maria's shrill voice called, "MOM?"

"She's not home yet," Johnny replied.

His little sister trailed through the room. Her purple jeans were so tight the top button had come undone and her outie bellybutton showed beneath her short pink top. Her curls were growing longer now and bobbed against her shoulders.

"When's Mom coming home?" she asked. "I'm hungry!"

Jonny shrugged, gripping his controller tighter. Maria was sorta cute, but she could be a pain too. Right now she was distracting him from winning the next level.

"There's wafer cookies in the kitchen," he said. She scampered off just as Dad stuck his head through the family room door.

"Hey there, kiddo," he said with a grin. He yanked his dress shirt out of the waist of his dress khakis and ran a hand through his hair. Now he looked rumpled and tired instead of pleated and crisp.

"Can we eat Thai tonight?" Jonny asked, but suddenly the front door swung open again.

A waft of salty, greasy spiciness curled right down the hall. It grabbed hold of Jonny's nose and sucked him out of his video game.

"Pizza!" he yelled happily.

"Pizza!" yelled Maria, running from the kitchen.

Mom laughed, shaking back her long hair as Maria barrelled against her legs. Mom held the big pizza box high overhead. "Baby, let me go!" she said. "We need to eat this food while it's hot!"

Jonny hit the pause button and ran to fetch plates from the kitchen cupboard. This was his favorite time of day...the time when Steve's gang and the silence and the hunger in his belly all shrank so small they didn't even matter.

Chapter Three

Game Over

For the next two days, Jonny managed to avoid Brenda Sloten on his morning and afternoon walks to school.

In the mornings, he left extra early and hurried along as fast as possible so as to stay ahead of her. By the time he reached school, his shirt was sticking to his back with sweat despite the cool morning air. Then he was faced with the problem of how to hang around outside school without getting cornered by the gang anywhere near the dumpster. Or behind the buildings. Or in the shadow beside the entrance steps. Or even behind a tree.

He solved the problem by hanging around where the buses stopped. Here he was almost constantly surrounded by students. This wasn't totally great because he kept getting shoved or even accidentally hit by heavy backpacks. Also, he'd have preferred not to get too close to anyone at all, because he was worried about his sweaty shirt and what names he might get called if anyone sniffed at it. The name smelly pig seemed like a possibility.

In the afternoons, Jonny tried to use a reverse policy and escape from school ahead of Brenda. But she seemed to have a way of getting out of the yard very fast. Twice, he found himself stuck behind her. Man, did she walk slowly once she was away from school! A snail could have beaten her without raising a sweat. She stopped to look at things, like dried flowers and bushes with leaves turning red. She talked to dogs on leashes. She picked up cats and cuddled them. She picked up dead leaves and looked at them; some she even slipped into her backpack. She was sorta weird – but mainly, she was plain aggravating. Lurking along behind her in gateways and shadows, Jonny thought, Hurry up, hurry up, for Pete's sake. I want to play with Shadow! And I'm starving! Maybe Mom bought some more of that cookie dough ice-cream with sprinkles.

His stomach grumbled and pinched. Still, Brenda sauntered along in her stripy yellow and pink ruffled top and her yellow jeggings. Her sandals flapped against the pavement. Her toe nail polish was purple. She hummed a little as she watched a late butterfly searching for any remaining flowers. While she hummed, Jonny sweated. He had to get a move on before the gang found him out here in a danger zone. He had to get home!

Brenda was making life complicated.

At the beginning of the next week, Jonny got a break. Pete was off sick, and Liz was busy playing with her new phone. She texted all through English class. "If you don't put that gadget away, I will," the teacher, Ms. Singh, finally threatened. "I'll put it away in my desk drawer and lock it."

Liz pouted. "I thought you'd be happy I'm WRITING things and using the English language," she said.

"I am not sure that text words even are the English language," Ms. Singh replied. "Perhaps you'd care to step up to the board. Give us some examples of how your texting is changing the English language."

Liz's pout turned to a look of shock as the teacher held out the chalk.

"Well, come on then. We're all waiting for your lesson," Ms. Singh said.

Liz stomped past Johnny's desk in her new suede boots. The heels were made of things that looked like large screws. Liz shot Jonny a dirty look, and he quickly ducked his head and looked away. Now that Ms. Singh had put Liz in such a bad mood, Jonny would need to be extra cautious all day. Once again, he wished for a cloak of invisibility that could hide him from Liz and her friends.

In his video game, he'd finally won his cloak. After that, he'd rushed through the next two levels, safe under his cloak and with faithful Shadow warning him of enemy locations. Those two levels had been a blast, and Jonny's warrior-magician strength was growing by leaps and bounds. The warrior was a sinewy guy, broad but in a strong way instead of a fat way. He looked like he could climb mountains and toss rocks aside. He looked like a tree that had survived drought, flood, ice, and wind.

Kinda the way, in fact, that Dad looked in old family pictures. Dad used to be on the rowing team and the track team in college. His awards were gathering dust in the basement now. "Didn't always have this spare tire," he'd say, slapping his belly. "Nope, your dad was once an athlete."

Jonny was jerked back to the reality of the classroom by Ms. Singh. She had paused beside his desk. "Perhaps you'd like to share what you're thinking about?" she asked.

Jonny flushed with embarrassment. "Athletes," he mumbled to his chubby hands gripped together in his lap.

A couple of people giggled.

"Athletes!" snorted Steve in the back row. "Losers, more like. The only race that Jelly Fatsio will win is the hog race!"

"That will be another detention mark," said Ms. Singh, glaring at Steve. Behind her back, Liz wrote U R A LSR on the blackboard. She pointed the chalk at Jonny, and he felt all eyes in the class burning into him.

"Ms. Singh!" cried Brenda, flapping her hand wildly. Her fingernail polish was purple too.

"Yes, what is it?" Ms. Singh asked.

"On the board!" Brenda said, smiling that wide,

innocent smile she had.

Jonny stopped breathing. In fact, he wasn't sure if his heart was still beating. Brenda is telling on Liz?

Ms. Singh turned back to the board, but Liz had wiped it clean with one fast stoke. Quickly she scrawled TTYL. "This texting message means 'talk to you later'," she explained, waving the chalk in one hand. For a fraction of a second, the chalk paused in front of Brenda. Then Liz waved it on again. Did Brenda have a clue what a mess she'd just landed herself in? Jonny snuck a look towards her. Brenda was coloring flowers in the margins of her binder pages using a marker pen.

"You can return to your seat," Ms. Singh told Liz. At that moment, the bell rang for the end of class. Jonny couldn't get out the door fast enough. He crammed his books into his backpack and barged into the hallway. He had to get as far away from Steve and Liz and Brenda as possible. But somehow, Steve had gotten out the door ahead of him. He swung his foot between Jonny's legs. Jonny crashed forward, his head banging into a locker door. He sprawled on the floor, his books all sliding out though the pack's unzipped opening. So that was how he saw what happened next, because he had to sit there picking up his books.

First, Ms. Singh came out and walked away to the staff room. Then the rest of the students straggled out chatting and swapping sticks of gum and lip gloss and internet addresses. Then Liz sashayed out, her boot heels going tap tap tap. She stood beside Steve.

In a panic, Jonny heaved himself off the floor. He

bent to grab his backpack.

Brenda strolled out of the classroom, humming to herself.

"B. Sloten, isn't it?" Steve asked pleasantly, blocking Brenda's way. She backed up against the door frame.

"It's B for Brenda," she explained. Her wide face looked calm, but she started twisting strands of her long blonde hair around her fingers.

Liz tittered. "I thought it was B for Big," she said. "But I guess you know your own name."

Brenda flushed. "Let me go past," she said, but Steve didn't move. He just rested one hand on the doorframe so that the muscles in his arm were right in front of Brenda's nose.

"Like Liz said, I think we're going to change your name to Big," Steve drawled.

"And your last name...that might need changing too," Liz said.

"You are a totally big...a big fat -- what?" Steve pondered aloud.

It was Liz who was clever with words. "She's a Big Sloth," Liz said.

"Brenda Sloten. We hereby rename you Big Sloth," said Steve, and he flexed his arm muscles.

Even though he was five feet away, Jonny winced. Other than this, he didn't move. He was as still as a stone...still enough, he hoped, to be invisible. Part of him wanted to be a hero and to rescue Brenda. But he didn't have Shadow or any magic potion, and without them he knew he was not a hero. He was just a lumpy fat kid. He needed to find an outside door and get home fast before Steve and Liz swivelled their bad mood onto him.

In one swift motion, he raised his pack to his shoulder and panted away.

"No running in the halls!" a teacher called from a classroom. Gasping, Jonny slowed to a fast shuffle. He burst out into a misty rain and crossed the yard at a clumsy jog. His pack slapped his back. When he reached the street safely, he slowed down a little bit. His lungs burned and his eyes misted over with – something. Rain or sweat? His skin was definitely sweating, but it also seemed to be itching. Itching with shame. He couldn't believe he'd just left the new girl alone with the bullies, but he had.

At least, with them bullying her, they might leave me alone, said a voice in the back of his head.

Shut up! he thought in reply, but he knew it was possibly true. It was possible that he'd have things easier if the gang turned their attention to Brenda Sloten.

"Yoo hoo!" a voice called cheerfully. Jonny glanced over one shoulder and saw the wispy old woman being dragged along by her storm of dogs. He couldn't face her bright blue gaze. Even with all that mascara on her lashes, she'd see immediately what a total coward he was. He hurried on, head bent against the September rain.

At home, he turned the volume up higher than

usual and ate half a carton of cookie dough ice-cream and three chocolate cupcakes before he even changed from his wet clothes. Despite the food, his skin still felt itchy. To distract himself, he ate a small bag of chips and a little more ice-cream. He had a warm shower and pulled his favorite sweat pants up under his belly. His skin still felt like little spiders were crawling on it. He finished up the rest of the carton of ice-cream. Then he went to see if he could beat the game's next level.

Even though it was only September, he already knew that grade seven was going to be very messy. And last a very long time. He'd ask Mom to keep the cupboard well-stocked at all times. Otherwise, he might not survive.

Chapter Four

Weird Science

In October, Johnny's Biology teacher taught the class about animal hibernation. They learned about how an animal's body temperature dropped as winter approached. Animals getting ready to hibernate moved around more slowly and ate a lot. Bulking up on extra calories gave them strength to survive winter.

Sounds good to me, Jonny thought. Staring at his desk, he started to imagine that he was a grizzly bear. He was fearless, the king of the wilderness. He was bulking up, getting scarier and fiercer with every calorie. But the bear's growth was cut short by the bell ringing, and Jonny dragged himself off home behind Brenda.

After a dinner of fried corndogs and soda, served by Dad, Jonny went to his room. He spread his English homework on his desk. Mom was out selling a split-level ranch with a hot tub, and Maria was at a sleepover. Faintly, from the family room, Jonny could hear the roar of football on TV. Dad liked to watch it, yelling advice like he was a coach. When he got frustrated with players, he just roared.

Jonny worked his way through the English questions. His mind was getting tired. He decided that his lair needed supplies. He thumped into the kitchen and found a bag of jalapeno taco chips, a plastic bin of gummy worms, and a packet of chocolate cookies. It didn't seem like a great deal to feed a bear in need of extra strength, but it was a start. Sliding the stuff into his closet and draping some dirty tee shirts over it made Jonny feel calmer. It seemed easier to think when he knew there was a supply of food close by.

He wondered if there were any computer games where he could start off as one thing, say a human or an elf, and then morph into a bear. Not just any bear but a bear with super powers that could fight using kick buttfu moves. That would be epic.

Jonny frowned over his homework again. English was hard. Last year, in grade six, he'd complained about how hard it was to make a grammatical sentence. His teacher had smiled and said,"Why, Jonny, you're great at mixing things together to make something new. In Science class, you do this all the time. Writing is the same. You just take words and mix them together in different ways to make new sentences."

Jonny thought privately that she hadn't a clue what a strange comparison that was. There was no way that mixing up words resembled playing with glass beakers, powdered chemicals, and gas flames. But he had nodded politely and gone back to erasing his spelling mistakes. He erased so much that he tore holes in the paper.

Now, in grade seven, Science was called Chemistry, and English was even harder. Jonny stared at a question on the homework sheet. # 9: List an oxymoron and use it in a sentence. Jonny wrote: Steve is a moron. Then he tore that part of the page out of his homework binder and threw it in the trash. He stared at the blank paper that was left behind and waited for inspiration to strike. All that happened was that he thought about jalapeno chips.

He tore the taco bag open. Just the rustle of it tearing made him feel calmer. He munched on tacos and thought about hibernating bears growing sleepier, cooler, fatter. When the tacos were all gone, he thought maybe he'd take a nap. Just a quick one. Then he'd finish his homework. He curled up on his bed and pulled his fleecy blanket around his ears.

Someone was shaking his shoulder.

"Mmmnnph?" he replied. He shrugged the hand off his shoulder.

The fleecy blanket was jerked back, letting in a flood of white light. What was this, an interrogation? Jonny cracked his eyes open. Dad's face looked sort of crumpled and his hair was askew on one side.

"Jonny, get up! Your mom's had to leave early and I have to pick Maria up. You'd better get yourself off to school."

"School…but I'm just napping…I'm just…"

But Dad was just gone already, slamming the front door behind him. Jonny shook his head in disbelief. His nap had lasted all night! Maybe this was how bears felt. One moment they were curling up for a little nap and the next moment – bam! – it was spring again. Sleeping a lot might be one way to make it through the school year.

Jonny rolled out of bed. His blank homework book still lay open on his desk. Jonny stared from it to the pile of dirty laundry on his closet floor. He couldn't wear the clothes he'd been sleeping in. Could he? Nah. He flung clothes this way and that, searching for something clean to wear. A tee shirt landed over his computer screen. Dirty socks hit the wall. A pair of faded jeans might do? Jonny tore off his track pants and squeezed himself into the jeans. He sucked in his belly and yanked the zipper up, up, up again. Finally. He couldn't breathe properly, and it was hard to bend at the waist. But if he didn't get going he'd never make it to school ahead of Brenda.

He grabbed a handful of gummy worms, stuffed them into his pack on top of his cell phone, and headed for the door. Half way down the drive, he remembered his homework book and panted back to fetch it. Period one was English, which meant he had to write down an oxymoron in the next half an hour. He flung the tee shirt off his computer, booted up his search engine, and entered a search. Licking his lips, he scribbled the phrase a little bit big into his notebook. "A sentence?" he mumbled. His stomach growled unhappily, reminding him he hadn't had breakfast yet.

Mom says my sister Maria is only a little bit big even though she's getting fat, he scribbled. Slamming the book shut, he rushed outside with it. Out of habit, he glanced both ways along the street. Dang it! There was Brenda just strolling past his driveway in a bright purple, shiny jacket and a pair of black jeans with purple sequins. The sequins disappeared into folds of Brenda's legs then popped out again as she walked. For a moment, Jonny was mesmerized. He wondered just how big a fat roll had to be in order to make things disappear and reappear.

He shook his head and stood around the side wall of his house, out of Brenda's sight. When his stomach growled again, he stuffed his mouth with gummy worms and waited for his hands to stop sweating. Going to and from school always made him sweaty this year. He wondered if it was a medical possibility that the sugar in candy could prevent nervous perspiration.

Thinking of candy reminded him that Halloween was a few weeks away. His stomach clenched. Did he dare to go trick or treating this year? What if Steve and the gang ambushed him someplace dark? What if no one paid any attention to his hollering? People might hear but not understand his shouted pleas for mercy. People might think the noises were merely Halloween special effects. But if he didn't go out with a pillowcase, he wouldn't get his annual stockpile of candy bars. And if he needed sugar now to stay calm, he needed to get out on Halloween more than ever before.

Jonny glanced at his watch. Yikes! Four minutes before the bell! He searched for Brenda, but her winking rolls were gone. Hitching his pack on his back, he hurried stiffly down the front steps. His legs were having trouble bending in the tight jeans. He felt like a soldier marching in a black and white film as he hurried to school.

Maybe it was the fears about Halloween or the worry over his English homework or the weirdness of Brenda's sequins. Whatever caused it, Jonny did not notice his problem until it was too late. In fact, he didn't notice it at all until Steve made everyone in class notice it.

It happened when the English teacher, Ms. Singh, asked if anyone had an announcement to make before class started. She always did this because she believed that making public announcements made students develop confidence. Jonny thought that it probably made students feel stared at. But he didn't know for sure because he'd never made an announcement.

Today, Jonny was almost late. He was stowing his backpack under his desk just as Ms. Singh said, "Does anyone have an announcement?"

"Jonny has one!" Steve said.

Jonny straightened up. His brain felt confused, sort of like his thoughts were lying all over the floor. "I don't have an announce— "

"What announcement is that?" Ms. Singh asked.

"He wants to announce that he's wearing red underwear." Steve kept his face straight. Heads swivelled. Jonny felt a hot-cold flush, like an oxymoron, spread through him. What was Steve talking about?

"Left hip," someone muttered.

Jonny stared in disbelief. The seam on his jeans, on his left hip, was splitting wide open. A flash of bright cotton showed through. In horror, Jonny shoved himself into his desk, trying to pull the seam shut with his fingers. As his legs bent to fit beneath the desk, the seam gaped wider. Jonny gulped and bowed his face. The class erupted into laughter.

Ms. Singh smacked his desktop with a ruler. "Enough!" she commanded. "I said, that's enough! Steven, sit outside the principal's office. Liz, see me after class. Brenda, if you have an announcement, come and make it."

Johnny's stomach clamped and unclamped like a boa constrictor that hadn't been fed for a month. He couldn't look up. Brenda's announcement sort of washed over the top of his head. Waves of misery and words seeped into his ears.

Dang tight jeans, he thought. Nerdy red underwear. I told Grandma not to buy me underwear!

"…shelter," Brenda was saying. "Any volunteers…mumble, mumble…"

Someone passed a note in front of Jonny. Someone else let out a snort of laughter, but Ms. Singh stopped it with a glare.

"...especially dogs but also cats," Brenda was saying.

What the heck was she talking about?

Jonny gripped the hole in his pants and risked a swift glance upwards. Brenda's face was pink, and her eyes were shining with seriousness. "I really hope some of you might volunteer," she said. "I'll write the number on the board."

When Brenda turned to pick up the chalk, someone whispered, "The Big Sloth needs a volunteer to walk her to her desk."

Jonny swung his head around. Liz smirked at him. "Hot color," she mouthed.

Jonny dropped his head again. Why was Brenda talking about dogs? He stared from under his lids as she put a telephone number on the board. Beneath it, in swooping letters, she wrote: Woodside Animal Shelter needs volunteers.

Johnny's mind filled with dogs' waving tails. Shining coats. Hopeful faces. They all needed to be loved. To be fed.

Hiding his English book cover with one hand, Jonny scrawled the phone number on it, and sank lower in his seat. He wanted to ask Brenda more but he couldn't. Not now, not after such an epic humiliation. There was no way he was going to start a conversation with Brenda Sloten aka Big Sloth right under the noses of Steve, Pete, and Liz.

Especially not with Halloween coming soon.

Chapter Five

Man's Best Friend

After Brenda's announcement about the animal shelter, Jonny kept wondering what she'd really said. If only he'd been listening, instead of trying to keep his hip squeezed inside his pants where it belonged.

Once, he found himself standing behind Brenda in the cafeteria line. Did he dare risk speaking to her? A quick glance around showed him that Steve's gang hadn't yet arrived to claim their window table. Jonny cleared his throat. He coughed in the direction of Brenda's soft blonde curls dangling down her wide back.

"Um, I was just wondering..." he said in a low tone.

"Are you talking to me?" Brenda asked too loudly. She swung around, knocking her food tray into Jonny's chest. Her eyes looked startled but also hopeful.

At that very moment, Jonny heard the tap tap of

Liz's boots nearby.

He shook his head at Brenda as if he hadn't a clue what she meant. He could feel flustered heat rising up his neck. "I'll have a double-large order of fries," he called loudly to the cafeteria lady who was serving behind the counter. She raised her eyebrows but didn't say anything, just pursed up her mouth like the words inside it were sour. Jonny grabbed his tray and carried it to where Markus was eating the flat pizza that the cafeteria sold. It was so flat it looked as if it had lain in an intersection during rush hour. Markus didn't seem to mind. He was wolfing it down in between texting on his cell. Since Jason moved away, Markus was the closest thing to a friend that Jonny had. They were study partners in chemistry, and sometimes during the holidays they hung out in the school yard shooting hoops.

Jonny set his tray down and slumped into a chair.

"Wasup?" Markus asked.

Jonny squirted ketchup onto his fries and waited until his breathing slowed down. "You know that thing about the animal shelter?" he asked.

"Uh-huh."

"What was it about?'

Markus glanced up from his screen. "It's that place at the south end of Woodside," he said. "You know, that grey building by the lights?"

Jonny nodded. He couldn't actually remember paying any attention to the building before, but he was sure he could find it. He had a good sense of direction.

"They need people to come by and, like, help walk dogs and do something with cats," Markus said. "Brush them or whatever you do with cats."

Jonny chewed and nodded. Do they let just anyone walk a dog? he wondered. Or do you have to have special…I dunno…special skills or something? What kind of dogs do they have there? Maybe I should check it out. But what if Brenda goes there?

If rumor spread around class that he and Brenda were walking dogs together, he'd be one huge bully target. Impossible to miss.

Jonny's mind was beginning to feel like a rope in a tug-of-war contest. Halloween candy tugged one way. Fear of being bullied in the dark tugged back. Wanting to go and walk dogs tugged another way. Fear of being seen walking with Brenda tugged back.

It was exhausting. To just deal with the stress of it all, Jonny kept ordering double-large fries every day for lunch. It took two cans of soda, not just one, to wash down so many fries. Afternoon classes were sort of a blur after this; everything seemed slow and fuzzy and far off because Jonny was so sleepy. He doodled bears with kick buttfu moves in the margins of his books.

One afternoon after school, Jonny was lurking around the bus stand, mingling inconspicuously. He'd already seen Brenda head homewards so he knew he'd have to wait a while before he headed that way himself. Liz had been picked up in an SUV, and Steve was playing an away match on the basketball team. That just left freckled Pete to avoid. When Jonny spotted him yakking to some other kids, waving his skinny elbows around, Jonny decided to make a break for it. It was now or never.

He sidled past the kids waiting for their bus, hustled around the south corner of the school, and set off down Woodside at a determined pace. At first the skin on his neck crawled as he waited for Pete's footsteps behind him. After a block or so, he stopped listening so hard. Besides, Pete by himself was not as scary as Pete with Steve and Liz to have his back.

Across the street from the Woodside Animal Shelter, Jonny paused. He swiped sweat from his forehead and hitched up his pants. For half a minute, he couldn't decide what to do. Then he plunged across the street and made himself walk inside. Barks echoed behind walls. A smell of fur and disinfectant rushed up Jonny's nose. He blinked in the fluorescent lighting and shuffled to the reception desk.

"Hey kid," said a short man, looking around a computer screen. The man's bald head shone, but at the back, he had enough long hair to make a ponytail. "Can I help you?" he asked in a strange accent. Maybe he was a Brit.

Jonny's mouth went dry. A wave of dorkiness swept over him. When he shuffled his feet, his stomach growled.

"I heard you wanted people, like volunteers," he muttered. "You know, to walk dogs and stuff like that…"

He trailed off uncertainly, but the man smiled.

"We certainly could do with some help," he agreed. "Like dogs, do you?"

Jonny nodded. "They're awesome."

"Well, you come back with me and meet some dogs," the man said. He stretched a hand over the desk. "I'm Alvin."

Jonny wiped his clammy hand on his pant leg and Alvin shook his hand with a warm, firm clasp. Then Jonny followed Alvin through swinging doors into a pale green room lined with cages. Barking broke out, barking and whining and howling. The noise was deafening.

"Settle down, you lot," Alvin said with a chuckle. "I've brought you a new friend."

Jonny trailed along the rows of cages. Tails thumped. Wet noses shoved at the wire. Eyes shone at him, pleading for a run, a chase, a bone. For a friend.

Alvin stopped in front of a cage. "Now, here's a nice quiet dog who really needs some exercise," he said. "His last owner nearly fed him to death."

The large golden dog had a long thick coat that hung over his round sides. He looked at Jonny with eyes the color of Halloween caramels. His tail swished.

Jonny held his hand to the wire. The dog's tongue rolled out and swiped Jonny's skin.

"Love at first sight," said Alvin. "Before you can walk him, you'll need to do some paperwork. Take it home, tell us about yourself, get a parent's signature. Then bring it back tomorrow."

Jonny's shoulders slumped with disappointment.

Just for a moment, he'd been imagining himself and this dog playing Frisbee in the park one block south of the Shelter. He might not squeeze up enough courage to come back tomorrow with paperwork. It might be a day when the gang were shadowing him.

Alvin stared at him weirdly. "Have parents, don't you?" he asked.

"Sure." Jonny turned away.

"Let him walk today," said a voice. A scrawny old lady stepped out of an empty cage. She was holding a paper towel in one hand and disinfectant in the other. Her scraggly grey hair was knotted in a bandana. She sent Jonny a bright stare through her blue mascara. He was zapped by a jolt of recognition.

"I see this boy going home," she said. "I know where he lives. Let him walk a dog today and bring the paperwork back next time he comes."

Jonny's mouth hung open in surprise. She must be a volunteer here, he thought.

"Thanks!" he called as the woman scurried away to a trash can. She flapped one hand in a wave.

"Well, that's fine and dandy then, mate," Alvin said. He slid the latch open and the hairy golden dog stepped out. He seemed to be smiling at Jonny. His lips had pink frills along the edges. Alvin snapped a lead onto the dog's collar.

"Keep him on this," he instructed. "You can take him to the park. Here. You'll need these."

He fished a handful of plastic poop bags from one pocket and handed them to Jonny. He didn't really want to take them, but the dog made a sort of panting noise as if he was sighing. Jonny shoved the plastic poop bags deep into his own cargo pockets. Alvin handed him the end of the leash.

"Head out the back door here," Alvin said. He leaned on the door and suddenly the dog hauled against the leash. Jonny was dragged out into the noise of city traffic.

He didn't even remember to glance around for Pete.

The dog seemed to know the direction of the park. He waddled along, panting. His fat sides rolled under his fur. His toenails clicked on the pavement.

"If you were a bear, you'd be ready to hibernate," Jonny muttered.

In the park, the dog sniffed everything: lampposts, trash cans, bushes, dead flowers. "You're never going to get fit dawdling along like this," Jonny told the dog. "What's your name anyway?"

The dog grinned.

I could call him Shadow, Jonny thought. But it's kind of lame for a yellow dog.

He couldn't think of anything else right then. "Shadow!" he said, and the dog stopped and turned his head. He wiped his mouth slobber on Jonny's cargo pants. Jonny stroked the dog's head and his long coat. There were all kinds of lumpy tangles in it. "You need a brush," Jonny said. "You're getting dreads."

Shadow flopped down on the path, panting. "You're worn out already!" Jonny said. "How are you going to play Frisbee?"

He tried to remember where his old blue Frisbee had gone, the one he and Jason used to play with. It seemed like a long time since he'd seen it. But there were probably lots of things in his room that he hadn't seen for a long time. Things lurking in his sock drawer that he never opened because he kept his socks under his computer desk. Things buried in the bottom of his laundry hamper under his old Lego sets and the red underwear his grandmother had bought and that he was never, ever, never going to wear again.

He tugged at Shadow's tangled coat as he thought about the Frisbee. Then he noticed how the sun was setting behind the office towers in the city centre. Dad was there someplace, in his world of white marble and steel beams and glass. Maybe he was already climbing into his car to fetch some take-out and bring it home for dinner.

"Time to go," Jonny said. Shadow rose and padded slowly alongside as Jonny headed back to the Shelter. The dog didn't seem that crazy about going. Once or twice, he glanced up at Jonny like he was asking "Are you sure about this?" Then he looked resigned and padded on like he'd follow Jonny anywhere that Jonny went, even if he didn't think it was such an epic idea.

It made Jonny feel sort of bigger than usual, not bigger in a way that made bullies notice him but bigger in a good way. Like warrior big.

Chapter Six

Trick or Treat?

When Jonny was a little kid, he loved Halloween more than any other celebration. He loved the crisp smell of the air. The waxy smooth feel of candles and pumpkins. The scary cackles and shrieks echoing through the neighborhood. The stockpile of candy bars he kept in his closet. He and Jason used to dump all their candy onto the floor and sort through it and swap stuff. Jason didn't like red liquorice, and Jonny didn't like anything flavored like peanut butter, so they used to swap that booty right off the bat.

Now that Jonny was in grade seven, he'd noticed that everything was starting to seem different. Like he'd put on a pair of someone else's glasses and the world looked all – askew somehow. Not only looked but felt, smelled, sounded different. Only his sense of taste hadn't changed: corndogs, fried chicken, and hash browns all tasted as great as ever. Which was a relief, because how much change could a person handle all at once?

One thing that felt different now was Halloween. Jonny just couldn't muster up the same love for it. I might be getting too old to trick or treat, he fretted. I'm not a little kid anymore. Watching Maria try on her Barbie princess outfit made him feel bummed. He remembered when he and Jason were that age. They used to haul their gear on right after school. By the time it was really dark and they could go, their costumes were half worn out already.

But if I don't go trick or treating, I won't get my candy stash. Markus says that his parents are giving out three Hershey bars to every kid! I need to be there!

To take his mind off the problem of Halloween slinking closer, Jonny kept going down to the animal shelter. First though, he spent an evening filling out the paperwork. Some of the questions were dead easy to answer, questions like: Do you have a driver's license? and Have you ever been charged with cruelty to animals? As if anyone who had been cruel would answer that truthfully! But maybe, he thought, they have some way of checking up on the answers.

Some questions were a lot tougher and he had to write grammatical sentences that Ms. Singh would have approved of. The hardest question was: Tell us why you want to volunteer at Woodside Animal Shelter. Mom closed a house deal on her cell during the time it took to answer this question. I want to walk dogs because... Jonny wrote. He chewed his pencil and then continued. ...dogs are fun to be around and my special dog friend, Shadow, needs exercise so he can start chasing balls and catching Frisbees. He's an awesome dog who deserves to have fun!

Jonny took the paperwork for Mom to sign. Luckily, she was selling real estate from in the kitchen. So he was able to grab a carton of chocolate milk and a pepperoni stick while he waited for her to get off the phone.

"This is a wonderful idea!" she said when Jonny showed her the form and explained about volunteering. She signed with her usual large flourish. Her signature looked as if it had flowers hidden in it, or maybe clouds. "Now you're doing all this walking in the cold, you'll need extra snacks," she said as she laid down her pen. "What can I buy for you?"

"Doughnuts with sprinkles?" Jonny asked.

"You got it! Anything for my boy!" Mom tossed her hair back, laughing, and handed Jonny the papers.

Sometimes Jonny arrived at the shelter late, because he'd had to avoid Steve's gang. When this happened, Alvin already had Shadow leashed and snoring under the computer desk.

"Hey mate, here's your personal trainer," Alvin would say to the dog. Shadow would give a snoring grunt and open his eyes and smile. He always got up as fast as he could, which wasn't so very fast. His stomach seemed to weigh him down.

Once, when they were at the park and Jonny was picking up Shadow's poop with the bag Alvin had supplied, he felt like he was being watched. He swivelled around, but there was no one in sight. In fact, now that the leaves were falling fast and turning from red to boring brown, the park was often deserted. Jonny's breath puffed in front of his mouth. He had to hustle Shadow around the paths more quickly so he could get the dog back to the shelter before dark.

Then he himself had to face six blocks of darkness to reach the safety of home. He kept the doughnuts with sprinkles in a bag in his jacket and crammed them into his face as he rushed along. His ears seemed to hover off the sides of his head, listening for the pad of sneakers, the thump of army boots, and the tap of screw-heeled suede boots. Jonny wished that Shadow could waddle home with him, bumping against his legs.

Sometimes, Jonny would pass the old lady volunteer on his walks. Alvin said she was called Phyllis. She'd wave and yell "yoo hoo" cheerfully, and rush on with her pack of dogs. Once or twice, Jonny saw Brenda walking a spotted Dalmatian with a limp. He hurried Shadow in another direction. Luckily Brenda was easy to see from a distance because of her crimson jacket and sky-blue scarf with crimson flowers. Once, Jonny thought he saw Liz at the shelter, whisking out the back door. But he couldn't think why she'd be there. Besides, there were lots of very skinny girls in tight black jeans and hoodies around, and he didn't have a chance to check for boots. So it probably wasn't Liz.

Halloween was on a Friday this year. A few days ahead of time, the principal announced that students could wear their costumes to school on Friday, and that there would be a costume and talent show in the gym after lunch.

"That's totally freaking lame," Pete moaned behind Jonny.

Jonny had to admit that, for once, he agreed with Pete about something. For the rest of the week, he debated what to do. Call in sick? Wear street clothes? Wear a costume? But what could he wear? He ransacked his room and found a half-eaten bag of taco chips he'd forgotten in his sock drawer. He found a beat-up blue Frisbee in an empty box that had once held a Lego space station set. Yes! Finally, beneath the mattress, he found his Spiderman outfit from Halloween last year. It was a puzzle how it had come to be there. Since he'd told Mom that he didn't want the cleaning lady in his room anymore, things had lapsed into a state of chaos.

Like this will fit me now, he thought. He pulled the costume on, the thin fabric stretching thinner and shinier with every tug. Flipping the closet door open, he glimpsed himself in the mirror that hung on the reverse side. One glimpse was enough. Spiderman's webs were stretched thin as a spider's legs. They swerved out over rolls of flesh. They disappeared into other rolls of flesh. And he had thought Brenda's sequined jeans were bad! He groaned. This costume seriously sucked on him. He peeled it off and wadded it into a ball which he flung into the back of the closet.

Street clothes then. Or a cloak of invisibility. As if.

On Friday morning, wearing jeans and his Red

Sox jacket, Jonny barrelled down the driveway and onto the sidewalk. He was wondering if he'd have time to walk Shadow before he went out trick or treating, and what he was even going to wear for trick or treating. Maybe that furry brown blanket that Mom liked to curl up in to watch movies when she had the flu? He could turn it into some sort of grizzly bear thing? If he was well enough disguised, Steve and the gang wouldn't recognize him even if they tripped over him. He could buy a mask down at the dollar store during lunch break... This could work.

"Hey, wait up!" called a voice from behind him. He teetered on the edge of the sidewalk, still two blocks from school. Wait up?

You're kidding me! Is she nuts?!

He turned slowly and reluctantly. Brenda surged down the street. Instead of her usual flamboyant clothing, she was in a dark brown outfit. Some kind of homemade bow and arrows were slung around her back.

"Hunger Games," she explained.

For just a moment, her calm smile fooled Jonny into thinking that everything about the current situation was going to be okay.

"How come you're not wearing costume?" she asked.

He shrugged. "I'm more into flying under the radar."

"I see you walking that dog from the shelter," she said. "Roger?"

Roger! What kind of name was that for a dog? "No, he's called Shadow," Jonny replied firmly.

"Whatever. We should, like, walk the dogs together sometime so they could play. That Dalmatian I walk? She had to have toe surgery after some creep cut her nails too short and they infected."

"Gross," Jonny muttered uneasily. Thoughts of toenails, a talent show, and Halloween bullying were making his stomach churn. It was rolling like a cement mixer. They were only half a block from school now. He stared in every direction, searching for the gang.

"Roger, I mean Shadow, he needs a professional grooming," Brenda said. "His coat is matted up. But the groomer who volunteers for the shelter hasn't been able to come in for awhile. All the dogs are getting shaggy. Even my dog needs a bath. She has been getting chemo for cancer."

"Your dog?" Jonny asked.

Brenda stared at him. "Are you okay?" she asked. "Of course not my dog. The grooming lady has cancer. That's why she hasn't been in lately. Who are you like looking for anyway?"

"Steve and the others."

Brenda's eyes went blank like a cloud had gone over the sun. "Oh them," she muttered. Her mouth drooped and she started winding her hair around her fingers.

It was like a magic trick that conjured people out of thin air. Because right behind them, a voice drawled, "Lookie lookie who we have here."

Brenda froze like a frightened bunny. Walk fast, blend, run! shouted a voice in Jonny's head. But he couldn't just abandon Brenda. Not a second time. If it wasn't for her, he might never have got to know Shadow.

"Come on," he muttered urgently to her. But Steve had already stepped around them to block their path. Pete and Liz flanked him.

"It's the poop team," Steve said.

"It's the super pooper scoopers," Liz added. She blew a bubble of pink gum and snapped it like a rubber band. She was made-up to look like a Goth vampire. Jonny thought that she was looking very pale even for that. There was fake blood running down her face and dark rings under her eyes. Jonny wasn't sure if they were make-up rings or real rings. She'd been looking kind of peaky lately.

"You can't talk. You -- " Brenda started to say back to Liz.

Liz shoved her in the shoulder and Brenda's face flushed.

"Shut your mouth," Liz demanded.

"Leave her alone!" Jonny said.

Steve eyed him up and down. "Hey, Jelly Fatso, don't you know what happens on Halloween? Things – get – eaten! Aaaaarrrr!"

Jonny lurched backwards away from Steve's growling face. Pete snickered then turned to follow Steve as he and Liz tramped away.

"See you," Jonny gabbled to Brenda. He rushed

to the back of the school and ate a bag of popcorn from his backpack to get calmed down. He couldn't believe he'd actually put himself in the path of the bullies.

The popcorn seemed to help and by lunchtime, Jonny was able to eat two pizza slices, one order of fries, and a large soda. But by the time of the talent show, his stomach was churning again.

In another few hours it will be dark, he kept thinking. Then what?

The talent show was partly funny and partly corny – until the gang got on stage. Then it was purely scary. Steve was wearing a red wife beater tee and baggy pants and a whole swath of fake gold bling. He stood in the center of the stage with Liz swaying on one side and Pete doing a few dance moves on the other. They had a sound track of hip hop blasting through the gym. Jonny was a little surprised that Steve could sing so well but mostly he was in a state of shock. Steve flexed his boxing club biceps as he swaggered and rapped.

> I'm a lean mean fightin' machine
> Lookin' for some action on Halloween.
>
> Me an' my buds we're gonna be cool,
> On Halloween night us rude dawgs rule.
>
> I'm a lean mean fightin' machine!
> I'm gonna fight to rule the night on Halloween!

The gym erupted in cheers. Steve's eyes roamed the crowd. They zeroed in on Jonny. "YO!" Steve shouted. "I'm talking to you! Know what I mean?"

Jonny slid down against a wall and hid behind a forest of legs. His own legs felt like jelly, just like the gang called him. Clutching his head in his hands, he thought, I'd have to be all-out majorly crazy to walk through the neighborhood tonight. Am I going to do it or not?

Chapter Seven

Fright Night

Thanks to the talent show and all the weirdness of Halloween costumes being worn at school, Jonny was able to make a super speedy get-away when the last bell rang. He jogged across the yard and squeezed through the gate. As he hurried towards home, neither the gang nor Brenda was anywhere in sight.

I'm not going out tonight, no way, Jonny thought as he panted along. I'll stay home and beat the next level.

Despite the chill air, he was sweating by the time he reached the front steps. He flung the door open and dropped his backpack with a crash against the leg of the table where Mom left her keys. They were there now, shining in the evening light.

Yes! Jonny felt a little better. If Mom was home, maybe the two of them could drink hot chocolate in the kitchen and snack on treats, while Dad took Maria around the block in her Barbie princess costume.

"Hey, Mom!" he called. "I'm home!"

"Come and look at me!" Maria shouted in excitement. Jonny went into the kitchen. His little sister was stuffed into a tight gown of sparkly blue fabric. Her brown eyes were shining brightly, and a fake tiara was perched on her curls.

"Mom's letting me wear some make-up!" Maria said with a giggle.

Mom glanced up from the items strewn on the countertop of the kitchen island.

"Hey there, sweetheart," she said. "Hungry? There's a tray of brownies in the fridge."

She bent over Maria and started brushing pink rouge onto her cheeks. Maria giggled as the brush tickled. Jonny's chest felt loose and long, like a stretched-out elastic band. Mostly nowadays it felt so tight that he could barely breathe. Today had been totally messed up but now everything was going to be okay. Jonny reached into the fridge and pulled out the tray of brownies, frosted in mint icing, and a can of soda. Perching himself on a barstool, he watched Mom and Maria.

"So, kiddo," said Mom, straightening up, "what are you going out as this year?"

"Nah, I'm too old for this little kid stuff," Jonny said. "I'm going to stay home this year and like, you know, work on some homework or something."

Mom widened her eyes in surprise. "No kidding? I've got your pillow case ready!"

"Well, I just think I'm getting too old for this stuff," Jonny replied. He slurped hard on his soda, avoiding Mom's eyes and hoping she'd buy his story.

"I'm ready now!" Maria said. "Mom, can we go now? Can we?"

Mom reluctantly tore her gaze away from Jonny as Maria tugged at her pants. "Honey, we need to wait until it gets dark," she explained. "Then Dad will be home to take you. He'll be your knight in shining armour!"

Maria giggled and rushed off to the family room, her feet thudding on the carpet.

Jonny cut himself another brownie square and took it to his room. As he turned on his game, he heard the phone ringing. After a few minutes, it rang again. Then his door opened and Mom poked her head in.

"Jonny, I'm really sorry, but I need your help," Mom said.

He paused the game and swivelled to look at her.

"Dad called and he's been held up in a meeting so he might be late home," Mom explained. "And I've just had a client call and they want to write up an offer on a condo. It's a big deal so I don't want to lose it. The client is in a hurry. So...would you mind taking Maria out trick or treating?"

Jonny's heart dropped like a stone and thudded against the bottom of his stomach. His chest tightened. An image of Steve, draped in bling, flashed through his mind. He could hear Steve rapping: I'm a lean mean fightin' machine! I'm gonna fight to rule the night on

Halloween!

"But Mom – I have all this, like, homework…and I'm too old for this kid stuff. I can't –"

Mom held her hand up. "Jonny, Maria will be super disappointed if you don't take her out. It's only for an hour. Then Dad and I will be home with take-out and we'll all have dinner. C'mon, do it for your little sister?"

Jonny squirmed in his chair.

"How far do I have to go with her?" he mumbled.

"Just around a couple of blocks. It won't take you long."

"This is lame," Johnny said. "Can't your client wait?"

"Jonny, you know we're saving for a trip to Bermuda next spring. I thought you wanted to go snorkelling. If I sell this condo, we'll be closer to affording our trip."

Jonny nodded. He'd have to cave.

"Okay, I'll take Maria."

"That's my boy! Bermuda, here we come!"

Mom flashed her dazzling smile and rushed away with a toss of her hair. Jonny heard the jingle of her keys, and then the sound of the front door closing. A heavy feeling of dread settled over his shoulders.

Snorkelling, he thought grimly. I'll be shark bait if I go outside tonight.

He swivelled back to his game and let it suck him away into a world of dwarves and mountain tunnels. His faithful Shadow crept at his side as they came closer to the throne of the Underworld King. Jonny's hands sweated on the controllers. He held his sword high.

Suddenly Maria burst into his room. "It's dark out!" she said. "Come on, Mom says you have to take me when it gets dark out."

Jonny sighed. "Wait, I have to beat the level," he said. But I need to get Maria around two blocks and then home before it gets any later!

A jolt of energy made his heart race.

"Okay, we'll go now," he agreed. Rushing through the kitchen, he grabbed a handful of mini candy bars and stuffed them into the pocket of his jacket. Then he helped Maria drape a fake fur shawl over her shoulders. "Don't crinkle my dress," she instructed.

"No way," he agreed, taking her hand. Together they started off along the road amongst scattered groups of other young trick or treaters. Jonny swivelled his head, searching for gang members but he only saw little Supermen, vampires, ghosts, and pirates. Maria's pillowcase bumped against his knees as he carried it for her. Her tiara had slipped to one side, and her make-up was smudged, but her eyes were sparkling. Jonny had to admit that she looked cuter than usual.

At the far end of the second block was a small park with winding paths and benches amongst the shrubs.

"Now we're going home," Jonny said when they reached it.

"But my best friend lives over there!" Maria pointed to the far side of the park. "And I promised we'd come to her house. If I don't come, she won't be my friend any more."

"Then she's not a very good friend to start with," Jonny said.

"But I promised," she said. Maria could be very stubborn for someone so small.

"Too bad, we're not going." Jonny tugged at her hand, but Maria planted her feet apart and refused to budge.

"I said, we're not going there."

Maria's lips trembled and her chin wobbled. She was about to let out a shriek. She had a very loud shriek for someone so small.

Jonny sighed. He thought, We can cross the park in five minutes. Be back here in ten minutes max. No problem.

"Aww, don't cry," he told Maria. "We'll go to your friend's place but that's IT! Then we're going home. Okay?'

"Okay." Maria's hand gripped his and they hurried through the park. So far, so good. But at Maria's friend's house, the mom wanted them to come inside, meet the family, and drink hot chocolate. Jonny slurped his down too fast, burning his tongue.

"Come ON," he hissed at Maria. "We have to go NOW!"

She huffed on her drink. "It's too hot," she complained. Jonny waited while she sipped it slowly, slowly. He was so worried and uptight he wanted to just grab it away from her. Now she didn't look the least bit cute. She was a totally aggravating little kid.

Finally, she finished her drink and Jonny hustled her outside. It seemed darker than before. The street lights were casting pools into the park's darkness. Between the pools of light were scary shadows. The streets were quieter now; most of the little kids and their parents had gone home.

Jonny dragged Maria along.

"You're going too fast," she protested. "Let me go!"

But he kept a firm grip on her hand as they plunged across the park. In the distance, Jonny could hear yelling and laughter. A dog barked. A car purred down the block and then there was silence again.

Jonny dragged Maria very fast past a clump of tall, gloomy pine trees. Ahead lay the grass with its climbing gym. The rusty creak of a swing chain sent chills down Jonny's back. He darted a glance towards the play area. Two figures were huddled near the swing set, and a girl in a hoodie was seated on one swing, her skinny legs dangling.

Jonny's pulse raced, slowed, raced on.

"Run fast!" he hissed at Maria and he yanked her forward.

"STOP YANKING ME!" she hollered.

The pillowcase Jonny was carrying, full of Maria's treats, swung between his legs and tangled him up. He stumbled and then crashed onto the gravel path. Candy bars fell out of the pillowcase all around him.

"Hey, it's Jelly Fatso!" said the voice of Pete the

Cheat.

Jonny's heart thundered in his ears. He struggled to his feet, hauling at the pillowcase.

"He's kidnapping a little girl," said Liz, jumping from the swing and making the chains creak again.

"We can't let that happen," drawled Steve. The three of them moved forwards. Jonny wanted to run, but he couldn't leave Maria. She was bent over, scrabbling to pick up her candy bars.

"Just leave them there!" Jonny told her.

"Maybe you should leave the little girl here," Pete said with a snicker.

"And her candy too. What are you doing anyway? Stealing a little kid's candy?" Steve blocked the path, his boots spread wide.

"She's my sister," Jonny gasped. "I have to take her home."

"I think she'd like a swing," Liz said. She squatted down level with Maria. "I bet you'd like a swing ride," she coaxed.

Maria looked uncertainly at Liz, then at Jonny. She knuckled one eye, smudging the mascara on her eyelashes. Now she looked like a raccoon.

"How about I give you a swing ride?" Liz repeated.

"Okay," Maria said. She started to follow Liz across the grass. Pete stooped and picked up one last candy bar and tore the wrapper open.

Panic wrapped its hands around Jonny's throat. He was being strangled to death! Dizzily, he tried to jump past Steve and chase after Maria. But Steve's reflexes were lightning fast. He was in front of Jonny again, his fists raised in a block. "Let the little girl have a swing," he said.

Over Steve's shoulder, Jonny saw Liz stalking away. She was having trouble on the grass. The screw heels on her suede boots were poking holes everywhere. She reached out and took hold of Maria's hand.

"Leave my sister alone!" Jonny shouted. "Maria, come back here!"

But Maria was being lifted onto a swing by Liz. Jonny had a sudden image of Maria being pushed higher and higher. With one final shove from Liz, Maria would get airborne, flying through the night, crashing into the darkness of the park, breaking her bones...

"NO!" Jonny shouted. He was determined to save his sister, no matter what. Like a mad bull, Jonny rushed at Steve, head down and hands clenched. He struck out blindly at Steve, but his fists met only air. Steve laughed. He dodged and danced while Jonny lumbered after him, flailing with both fists. He wasn't landing any blows.

The beam of a flashlight pierced the park. "What's happening over there?" a voice demanded. The flashlight bobbed closer.

"Split, split!" Pete called urgently. He rushed away into the night. Jonny saw Steve's eyes roll. The fake bling glinted in the street light. "I'm a fightin' machine," Steve snarled. "But you're a fat loser. So long."

Steve's fist drove into Jonny's stomach. He doubled over with pain, retching. A yell broke from his mouth. His legs staggered. Steve's second blow smashed into Jonny's face. He pitched forward onto the grass. His ears rang. Flashes of white pain knifed through his left eye and into his brain. He drooled and sobbed for breath.

Maria, Maria, I have to get to Maria.

He forced himself to his knees, but a wave of dizziness held him there. The grass and trees swung circles around him.

Moaning, he forced himself to stand.

He peered around, trying to see through one eye. Was the left eye blinded? It wouldn't open! Was he going to be blind for the rest of his life?

·The figure with the flashlight had almost reached the swing set.

Who is it? I have to save Maria!

Before Jonny could move, the figure with the flashlight reached Liz. The light swooped around as the figure swung its arm. "Get out of here!" a voice yelled. "I've called the cops on my cell phone. Get out and leave the little girl alone!"

Liz's white face tensed with fear. She let go of the swing and leaped away. Maria began to wail loudly.

Jonny forced himself to move, clutching his side, and still fighting for air. His lungs seemed to have collapsed with pain. His feet crunched on gravel. Light gleamed on the red and blue paint of the swing set. Jonny grabbed at the solid, cold metal and steadied himself.

The flashlight beam swung around onto him, blinding his one good eye. Fresh panic surged through him.

"Oh it's you," said the same voice that had called out before, asking what was going on.

Finally Jonny recognised it. "B –Brenda?" he stuttered.

"It's me." Brenda pulled the swing to a stop and tucked the flashlight into the quiver of arrows on the back of her costume. "Don't cry," she said gently to Maria. "Everything is okay now." She hugged Maria and patted her on the back. Maria hiccupped and whimpered.

"Did you really call the cops?" Jonny asked.

Brenda snorted. "I don't even own a cell phone," she said. "Are you okay?"

"I guess. My eye won't open."

"You'd better get cold water on it. Let's get Maria home. I'll carry her. Can you bring the candy?"

Jonny nodded, his head still swinging dizzily. He fumbled on the pavement for Maria's pillowcase and then stumbled after Brenda. Her shadow joined to Maria's shadow was huge as it moved away across the pale grass. Jonny followed, squinting, fingering his eye. It felt as round and tender as a ripe tomato. At least it didn't seem to be oozing any blood.

Brenda was panting as she carried Maria. It was amazing that she could carry her at all; Maria was packing on the pounds lately.

"I bet she can walk from here," Jonny said as they reached Carambola Circle. Brenda set Maria down gently and smoothed her crinkled dress.

"My tiara is lost!" Maria cried, her lips trembling again.

"We can go back and find it tomorrow," Brenda said. "You can help me walk my dog, and I'll help find your tiara."

"Um...thanks," Jonny muttered as he took Maria's hand. "Thanks, Brenda, you were great."

"No problem. See you around." Brenda turned and trudged away, and Jonny led Maria home.

How am I going to explain this eye to Mom and Dad? he wondered as he went up the front steps.

Chapter Eight

Nothing But The Truth

"Don't say anything about-- " Jonny started to tell Maria.

But just at that moment, Dad swung the door open. He must have heard them coming up the steps.

"Jonny got beat up!" Maria shouted.

Dad's cheerful grin flipped itself upside-down into a scowl of horror and surprise. "Holy shmoly!" he exclaimed "What happened to your face?"

"It's not too bad," Jonny said, trying to sound casual. "I just sort of fell over and banged it."

"He was punched!" Maria said.

"Who punched you?" Dad asked sternly.

Mom's face suddenly appeared by Dad's shoulder. "Good grief!" she said. "What's going on? You need ice for that swelling! Come into the kitchen."

Everyone followed Mom down the hall. Jonny dumped Maria's pillowcase onto the counter. "Look how much stuff she got!" he said. "That old lady at the end of the block? She gave Maria three packets of red liquorice and -- "

"Hold this against your face," Mom said. She handed Jonny a tea towel wrapped around crushed ice. When he held it gingerly against his skin, the burn of the ice distracted his brain from the real cause of the pain.

Which was more than he could say for his diversionary tactics about candy. His dad wasn't going to get distracted by red liquorice or any other kind of treat.

"I want to know what's going on," Dad said. ""Everybody sit down. We're going to get to the bottom of this."

Jonny's heart sank. Now Mom would fuss and Dad would scowl and everyone would know that he was just a walking lump of cowardice and misery and fat cells.

"Who beat you up?" Dad asked.

Jonny shrugged. "Just some kids," he muttered.

"Kids from school?" Mom asked. Great, now he had two interrogators.

"I guess."

Mom and Dad flashed each other a glance. Jonny wasn't sure what it meant, but he'd learned long ago that Mom and Dad could say all kinds of things to each other with just a flick of their eyeballs. You'd think they'd trained for it especially. Maybe at a Parenting class before he was born.

"Nobody is leaving this kitchen, and nobody is eating any candy, until you tell us what's going on," Dad said.

Mom lifted the pillowcase of treats and chips and stuffed it into a cupboard. Maria pouted and swung her legs, dangling off a barstool, but stayed silent.

Jonny took a deep breath. "There's this gang," he said. "Steve the Peeve and Pete the Cheat and Liz."

"They give you trouble before?" Dad asked.

Jonny nodded. "But not this bad. They usually just say stuff."

"Sticks and stones will break your bones, but words will never hurt you," piped up Maria.

"That old saying is a load of horse manure!" Mom said angrily, her cheeks flushing. "Mean words can cut your heart up! Mean words can leave you feeling bruised and beaten!"

Mom and Dad flashed each other another glance.

"We're visiting your principal tomorrow," Dad said. "We'll get this sorted out."

"No!" Jonny muttered. Could his night get any worse? If the gang knew he'd caved in and squealed on them, they'd take revenge. School would only become worse…Jonny didn't think he could face it. His head throbbed worse than ever, pulsing and hot.

"What are these words they say?" Mom asked.

"Dunno. Just stuff."

But Mom and Dad wouldn't let up; they should have worked for the FBI. They ground Jonny down with questions until he finally confessed that the gang thought he was a fat loser, a fatty, a hulk, a hippo, a chubby, a jelly. With every word that he repeated, Jonny felt himself growing heavier and stupider, a clumsy no-good waste of space. He wouldn't have been surprised, right in that dark moment of shame, if his parents showed him politely to the front door and told him they didn't want to even be his parents anymore.

But of course, they didn't do that. After Jonny finished talking, there was a long silence in the kitchen. Dad rumpled his hair. He paced and scowled, deep in thought. Mom chewed her lip and blew her bangs off her forehead and twisted her rings.

"There are going to be some changes around here," Dad said finally. "I'm going to buy a Wii. You're spending too much time on the couch playing video games. Son, you and I are going to play Wii together. We'll both get slim and trim. It'll be fun!"

He sent Jonny a look that told Jonny he needed to agree. Jonny shrugged his shoulders.

"From now on, I'm buying you only healthy snacks," Mom said. "And no more soda."

"Aww, MOM!" Maria and Jonny moaned together.

"We'll cook together as a family and eat together," Mom said. "I won't be available for work in the evenings."

"What about Bermuda?" Jonny asked. Suddenly, snorkelling away into clear blue water seemed like the most brilliant idea he'd ever had. No kids. No school. Just flashy fish and a wide-open horizon. Heck, being fat might even be an advantage; he'd have all that blubber to buoy him up. He'd barely have to swim, just drift along like a young whale. Drift and forget about names and bruises.

"We'll still try to go for vacation," Mom said. "It might just take us longer to save up."

Longer...Jonny repeated the word dismally inside his head. I can't take all this much longer...

"Off to bed," Dad said.

By half-way through the next afternoon, Jonny knew for sure that Mom and Dad had kept their word and visited the principal. Between chemistry and phys ed class, Steve accidentally on purpose shoved him into his own locker door. The chips Jonny was eating disintegrated into little bits in his hand as he lurched against the metal.

"Fat squealer," Steve whispered against his ear. "You'll pay for this."

Jonny had already been dreading phys ed class. Now he dragged his feet along the hall, not caring if he got detention marks for being late. He waited until everyone else had changed in the locker room and was out in the gym. He could hear the distant echo of basketballs bouncing and sneakers squealing on the polished wood. Slowly, he fumbled his clothes off and dragged on a baggy shirt and shorts.

Ms. McGee, the teacher, always bounced on her toes and looked fit in white. She glanced at Jonny as he slunk into the gym. "Ropes!" she called in her shrill voice. "One person climbing on the rope, one at the bottom to hold the end!"

Jonny lounged against a wall and tried to believe he was invisible. Maybe he should say that he felt sick. Which was true; his stomach was heaving. But Ms. McGee spotted him and blew her whistle.

"On a rope!" she commanded.

"I'll help you out there," said Steve, ambling by and grinning at the teacher.

"Up you go," said Pete, shadowing Steve.

Jonny stared at the long strands of smooth fibres hanging from high up near the ceiling. He grabbed the rope with both hands and slowly, painfully, hauled himself up, using the cross-ropes to place his feet on.

"Oops!" said Pete, swinging a spare rope across and flapping it against Jonny's ankle. Jonny lifted his foot. Wrong move. Pete flapped the rope around his ankle. Panic beat in Jonny's chest.

I'm going to crash to the floor!

Steve gave the end of Jonny's rope a swing and a tug. Jonny lifted his other foot to climb up higher. Steve's rope flapped beneath his foot and, quick as a cowboy roping a steer, Steve wrapped that rope twice around Jonny's leg. Jonny put his foot down on a cross-rope. Then he froze. He didn't know what to do next.

Climb down! yelled a voice in his head. But when he obeyed, Steve and Pete somehow jerked on their ropes and before he knew it, Jonny's hands were slipping. His feet kicked at air. For one horrible moment, he dangled upside-down. Ropes squeezed his ankles. Blood rushed to his head.

"Aw, poor guy, he's hog-tied!" Steve shouted, his words echoing off the gym walls. Students laughed and giggled. Jonny's face flamed red.

"Help him down immediately, and stop this goofing around!" Ms. McGee demanded.

Steve climbed alongside as Jonny hauled himself right way up. "Too bad we couldn't roast you on a spit, you little suckling squealing pig," Steve muttered as he helped Jonny get free of the ropes. Jonny didn't reply. He slid down as fast as he could, his feet thudding onto the floor.

He knew Mom and Dad had been trying to help, but he also knew that things were not going to improve at school. Not unless he did something about the problems himself. But what? What could he do? Solving his problems seemed like a fantasy – a fantasy like being able to play on the basketball team or swim in Bermuda. A fantasy like knowing how to cook fancy foods that didn't come already made, inside boxes, and ready to nuke. Nope, he wasn't likely to be able to do any of it.

At home, Mom kept her promise to be around more in the evenings. One night she made lasagne, and once Dad grilled burgers even though it was already getting cold outside. One night, the family went to Jonny's favorite Thai restaurant and he ate grilled chicken with lemon grass. What is lemon grass anyway? Is it really grass? Jonny wondered as he wolfed his food down. It would be cool to know how to make delicious meals, mixing up all the different stuff like mixing up stuff in chemistry class and making something different from it all.

Mostly though, even though Mom was home more, Dad brought them take-out for dinner. At first, he didn't bring any sodas with the food because Mom had given him strict instructions to go easy on the canned beverages. "Too much sugar," she said. But gradually they all got tired of drinking bottled water, and gradually Dad slipped right back into buying sodas again. Jonny didn't say anything – he didn't want to jog Mom's memory – so he just chugged the bubbles down.

Dad took him shopping one weekend and they bought a Wii and a bunch of games. At first, they had fun playing tennis and fighting off swordsmen and shooting hoops. But it was hard work keeping up with so much activity. Since Mom had stopped buying candy bars and chips and cookies, there was no way to recharge all that lost energy. Jonny and Dad had to flop on the couch, panting and sweating, and watch sports

on TV for awhile to get their strength back. And if Dad
was too busy to play, Jonny didn't bother. He felt like a
nerd thumping around in the family room on his own.
He asked Markus over a few times to play, and that was
cool. We could get to be buddies, Jonny thought
hopefully. But Markus was on the basketball team and
had a lot of practice games so he couldn't come by very
often.

Walking Shadow was still the most fun. Jonny
pretty much gave up trying to avoid Brenda on these
walks. For one thing, Brenda had saved him and Maria
from the gang, so it would have been epically ignorant
to avoid her. For another, Jonny was so worn down with
the bullying that he didn't have any will power to avoid
her. And for a third thing, Shadow liked the doggy
company of Brenda's Dalmatian.

"What's he called?" Jonny asked Brenda the first
time they took the dogs around the park together.

"She's a female dog," Brenda said. "See how
she's not limping now? Her toes have totally healed!"

"What's her name?"

"Shade," said Brenda with a smile tugging at the
corners of her mouth. Her cheeks dimpled and just for a
moment, something shone in her eyes.

"Shade! Seems like a weird name for a dog."

"They didn't call her that at the shelter," Brenda
said. "Alvin called her Spots. But I was like, really,
Spots? It's so unoriginal. So I named her after my
favorite female American artist, Shade Reeves. Do you
like her stuff?"

"I've never seen it," Jonny admitted.

"Well, it's big flowers in bright colors."

"Like your clothes," Jonny said, glancing sideways at Brenda. Today she was wearing a shiny purple jacket. Purple and pink feathers dangled from her pierced ears. Earlier that day, during math class, Liz had whispered, "Take one fat girl, add in six colors, multiply by four, and you get Big Sloth looking like an accident in a freak art shop."

Now Jonny suggested, "You might not get noticed by bullies if you dressed more like everyone else."

Brenda's soft mouth sagged. "But these are the colors I like," she said. "At home, everything is very bright. My mom's an artist. We both like things to be colorful."

"What about your dad?" Jonny asked.

"We don't live with him. We don't even know where he is," Brenda explained. She tugged on Shade's leash and walked faster, surging ahead of Jonny. He waited behind while Shadow sniffed at the messages on dead plants. It was like Facebook for dogs, Jonny thought. It was Plantbook.

Brenda's pink jeans made a rubbing noise against her thighs as she strode on. Jonny let Shadow have a long sniff. He thought maybe Brenda needed a moment to chill on her own. He hadn't meant to upset her. He'd only wanted to help, just like Mom and Dad had wanted to help him.

He guessed that no one could really help Brenda except Brenda. Just like no one could really help Jonny except Jonny. If only they could both find some way to change their worlds. But how?

Chapter Nine

The World Wide Web

Just before Thanksgiving, Dad got all hyper because his old college was holding a class reunion. Jonny found Dad rummaging through boxes in a basement closet one evening.

"Whatcha looking for?" Jonny asked.

Dad yanked out some grungy sports clothes and dropped them onto a pile of other stuff.

"Those were my uniforms when I was on the college track team," he said. He bent over the box again. "Aha!" he cried, pulling out a gold-plated award and waving it in front of Jonny's face.

"Here it is! My rowing crew won this in the State finals. Man, did we make that boat move!"

Dad stared at the inscription on the award, rubbed his rounded stomach thoughtfully, and sighed. "I sure was fit back then," he said. Then his face brightened. "But guess what?" he asked.

"What?"

"My old crew is all coming back for the reunion. And we've got permission to take the rowing shells out on the river and go for a row. So, son, I thought you could come too. What do you think? Want to row upriver with the old guys?"

Jonny felt a wave of doubt weaken his knees. "Aren't they sort of tippy, those rowing shells?" he asked. "They look so long and skinny."

"They're fine," Dad said. "You'll be with the pros. It'll be a blast!"

The day of the reunion was misty. Dad bounded into Jonny's room at some horrible hour, grinning and saying," Today's the day! Up you go, son!"

Jonny groaned and pulled the blanket over his head. He'd been in the middle of a dream about himself and Shadow cleverly outwitting the Underworld King and beating the game's final and hardest level. Hardest was putting it mildly; the level was more like brutal to beat. Jonny had been staying up late, struggling with it, for a couple of weeks now. Even his cloak of invisibility wasn't winning him the game.

Gradually the smell of bacon and eggs drifted under the blanket. Jonny's stomach started grumbling at him. When he tried to ignore it, it just hassled him louder. Finally, with a groan, he rolled out and dragged on some clothes. The furnace didn't seem to have kicked in yet, so the air felt chilly.

Better wear my jeans with the flannel lining, he decided.

They didn't look too grubby, and the lining felt soft and warm. Jonny struggled with the waistband button, sucked in his gut, and slipped the button through the hole. Then he pulled a sweatshirt over his tee shirt and grabbed the hoodie that was draped over the end of his desk.

After breakfast, he and Dad drove across town. Bare trees clawed at the thick mist. Office towers rose into the gloom, and frost lay thin as icing sugar on the grass. "It'll burn off," Dad said.

"Isn't the river going to be cold?" Jonny asked.

"Well, we're not planning on swimming," Dad said. He sang along to the radio and kept ruffling up his own hair with one hand. Jonny grinned to himself. It was good to see Dad looking so happy. Maybe this rowing thing would be okay.

The college campus spread along both banks of the river, joined by a bridge. Ghostly pedestrians appeared and disappeared along it. The tires of Dad's car rolled over the brown leaves carpeting the parking lot. Banners swung overhead in the mist. Their bright purple and orange lettering read Welcome Class of 1997.

The parking lot was almost full already. Dad swung into a space and jumped out. He slung an arm over Jonny's shoulders, and together they toured the campus with its long pathways winding amongst the trees, its residences, and its glass-plated library.

"Maybe you'll come here one day," Dad said.

Jonny shrugged. He couldn't imagine adding more years onto the torture that was school. Who would choose, of their own free will, to be bullied by college-size people? Only a moron. And imagine trying to stay safe in these miles of hallways and pathways with their great ambush spots!

Dad squeezed his shoulders. "You can do it," he said. "You're a smart kid."

That's what he thinks. If I'm so smart, how come I can't deal with my problems?

"Maybe you'll do chemistry here," Dad said. "That's seems to be your best grade."

"I'd kinda like to be a chef, maybe," Jonny said. The words took him by surprise.

"I mean, I like cooking shows," he said. That sounded lame.

Dad pulled a puzzled face. "We don't really cook at home," he said. "Takes too long. But your mom and I are fine with you doing whatever you want."

They crunched over the leaves in silence for a few minutes. The path sloped downhill, and suddenly they had a view of the river. The mist was thinning, just as Dad had predicted. A mob of people crowded the bank, and the rising sun glittered on the water.

"Calm as a bath tub," Dad said with grin. He hurried downhill, with Jonny puffing beside him, and plunged into the crowd. Soon he was roaring and laughing, slapping other guys on the back. Jonny didn't mind the fact that he didn't know any of the guys or get their old jokes. He felt safe here in the crowd; no one knew him and no one was hassling him. He didn't have to do anything except listen and watch.

After a bit, Dad led him along the shoreline to the docks where the rowing shell glistened in the water. It was so skinny and long that it was hard to believe it could hold a team of muscled guys. The metal oarlocks gleamed and the paddles shone. Water slapped against the shell as people walked on the docks, making them bounce.

I'm too fat. I won't fit into the boat. This is gonna be an epic fail. In front of all these people. I can't do it."

"Here's your life jacket," Dad said.

"I don't really want to do this," Jonny said but Dad had turned away, talking to a friend. Dad seemed so happy that Jonny didn't want to disappoint him. He dragged the lifejacket on and strained the straps tight across his chest and belly. Now he could hardly move; he felt like a Great Blue whale, largest mammal on the planet. Although, of course, whales had no trouble surviving underwater. Jonny stared doubtfully at the river's dark surface slipping smoothly past.

Then Dad and his friends started getting into the shell, and a guy helped Jonny in near Dad. Then the boat was gliding out into the current, and the bank was sliding away. Too fast. Too far. Jonny gulped nervously. Sunlight sparkled on the drips of water from the oars as the team began to row. Dad and the guys showed Jonny how to work his oar, and slowly, he got into the rhythm. After a few minutes, he forgot about everything except rowing. It was cool! The shell shot along like a giant water creature. The oars dipped and swung. Jonny's lungs sucked at misty cool air. One tree, still hanging onto its leaves, burst into bright red as the sun touched it.

This is awesome! Jonny thought. I can see why Dad liked it! Maybe I could row if I went to college...

They went upriver for a mile and then turned and shot back down. Jonny was starting to sweat inside his layers of flannel and fleece. As they approached the campus, Jonny saw that the crowd along the bank had grown larger.

"Rah, rah, River Rats!" some people shouted.

Dad grinned. "That was our crew nickname," he said.

At the dock, the crew climbed out. Dad wanted Jonny to stay put so he could get a photo of him. "Dang it!" he said. "I left the camera in the car. Just sit tight while I get it."

Jonny nodded. He watched Dad jog away into the crowd. After he'd sat in the shell waiting for a few minutes, a crowd of ladies came down the dock.

"We were the women's crew," one lady told him. "We're going to take the shell out and see if we still remember what to do."

"I'll get out of your way," Jonny said.

But how? He inched his rear end off the seat. The shell rocked and ripples lapped the dock.

"I'll steady it," one lady said, squatting and grabbing the edge of the shell. Hesitantly, Jonny shifted his weight off the seat and crouched in the bottom of the shell. He licked his lips. Then he slowly straightened his knees and took a step towards the dock. He was almost there.

The lady holding the boat turned her head away, laughing at something someone else was saying. The shell shifted. Jonny's weight shifted.

"Help me!" he shouted. But it was already too late.

He crashed headfirst towards the dark river. The shell flipped over, its wet hull shining. Jonny was flung out. He hit the water in a massive belly-flop. Icy cold darkness shocked through him. He wallowed and flapped his arms. Wet flannel and fleece dragged him down, but the life jacket bobbed him back to the surface. His eyes stung and streamed with water. He couldn't see anything except blobs of faces.

Everyone's staring. At least no one knows who I am. My legs are numb. COLD…COLD. I've gotta get out!

Jonny blinked and swiped water from his eyes. His hair felt glued to his forehead. Now he could see the women on the dock; they were dripping with water and the dock was soaked. He must have thrown up a ginormous splash when he hit the water. He'd never manage to climb onto the dock, although the women were all holding out their arms to him. He'd probably flip the whole thing over and dunk all the women's team, too.

He trod water for a minute, and then headed for the gravel shoreline. The crowd parted as he staggered out of the river. He smelled like seaweed, and his legs were so cold he couldn't feel them. They sagged like cooked spaghetti as he tried to walk up the bank. A couple of guys hoisted him by the elbows.

"You okay, kid?" one asked kindly.

Jonny tried to reply, but his face muscles were doing a complicated shivering that was making his teeth break dance. And his jaw had seized into one position. Maybe he had lock-jaw, whatever that was. For sure, he probably had hypothermia. He staggered on, searching for Dad, trying to drag the lifejacket off. The buckles were tight as vice-grips. And his fingers were white and shrivelled like they'd been underwater a long time. Dead man's fingers.

Jonny made it all the way to the parking lot before he found Dad leaning on the car, chatting to another guy.

"Holy mackerel!" he said when he saw Jonny. "What happened to you?"

Jonny's head jerked with cold. Dad unsnapped the lifejacket and hauled it off over Jonny's hoodie. "Take this back to the dock for me, would you?" he asked the other guy. Then he unlocked the car. Jonny climbed in with a squelching noise. His jeans oozed water. His hands steamed when Dad started the engine and turned on the heat.

"But I don't understand what happened," Dad said.

"I don't want to talk about it," Jonny muttered.

But it seemed that other people did want to talk about it. Because after Jonny got home and had a hot shower, the phone rang.

"Hey, dude," said Markus. "You okay?"

"Sure," Jonny said. Why's he asking me this? Jonny gripped the phone, his chest tightening.

"Cool," Markus said. "But I thought I should warn you. You might want to check out Facebook. About the boat thing?"

"The what?"

"The boat thing at the college this morning. Pete's uploaded some pictures. I wanted to warn you."

"The-thanks, man."

Jonny stumbled to his room. Mom had put a cup of hot chocolate with marshmallows on his desk. He pushed it aside and logged into Facebook.

Not just pictures. A video.

In the grainy images, Jonny watched himself trying to get out of the rowing shell. He looked massive, wrapped in layers of clothes and the lifejacket. He looked like Godzilla towering over the dock. No wonder the lady hadn't been able to steady the boat. Just his stomach probably weighed more than her whole body!

Over and over, Jonny watched the boat flip. The wave of water that his own body flung into the air. The ladies on the dock shrieking and jumping. Then there he was, floundering in the water, hair all over his face, arms flailing. There he was staggering ashore like a swamp hulk.

American tsunami caused by obese boy read the caption to the video.

Jonny's head sank to his desk. He felt beaten to a pulp by misery and shame.

He thought, I should have just stayed in the river and drowned.

Chapter Ten

What Time Is It?

Thanksgiving and Christmas passed in a blur. Jonny dragged himself to school. He closed his ears to the snickers and trash talk about his video splash. He took notes in class but afterwards he had no idea what he'd written down. Markus sometimes sat with him at lunch, and sometimes Brenda sat with him too. But he didn't feel like talking to them. He just wanted to eat. Luckily, it was the best time of year for eating. Jonny ate everything he could get his hands on: sweet stuff, salty stuff, greasy stuff. When he was eating, he didn't feel his problems. His pain went numb.

"Aren't you walking Shadow anymore?" Brenda asked one day in the cafeteria. Jonny shook his head.

"That dog, like, seriously needs a grooming," Brenda said. "I hope the groomer for the shelter comes back soon."

Jonny shrugged and ordered his food. He didn't

care anymore about Shadow's matted coat. Caring took way too much energy, and he had to hoard every ounce just to survive. Never mind dog shelters, he wished he could hide out in a people shelter, some place where he'd get fed and have nothing to do. Which was pretty much what home was over the Christmas holidays. Mom bought extra treats, and Jonny ate and ate. He drank eggnog and Coke. He ate eggnog flavored ice-cream. He ate chocolates and mashed potatoes and chips and cheese balls and corn dogs and pizza. He ate until even Mom began to tut-tut about the size of her grocery bill. Jonny ignored this. He and Dad watched lots of TV sports. Jonny didn't return Markus's phone calls asking if he wanted to play Wii together, and he didn't bother trying to beat his X-Box game's final level. It was too freaking hard. And who cared about a dumb make-believe wolf called Shadow anyway? He wasn't a little kid anymore. He was just a miserable, sad, muddled…nobody.

In January, on the second day of school, the principal made an announcement over the PA system.

"Listen up, students of Woodside!" he crackled. "Today there will be a special presentation in the gym, and I will see you all there! We're going to learn about healthy eating and getting fit!"

Whatever, blah, blah, Jonny thought. He was sitting in the back row in English, trying to sneak pieces of chocolate out of his cargo pocket and into his mouth.

Ms. Singh sighed and closed the book she'd been reading aloud from. "We'll talk about metaphors tomorrow," she said. "You can go to the gym now."

Jonny jammed his books into his pack and hauled it along to the gym. He was one of the last students to arrive, and he slumped against the back wall. Markus, nearby, shot him a grin. On stage, Jonny was surprised to see a bunch of guys dressed in street clothes. This was about food?

Suddenly music blasted through the gym and the guys began dancing. They were fit! Even Jonny sat up straighter and stared at their moves. Those guys could cover the floor! They could run up walls and flip somersaults! Students began clapping and swaying to the beat.

After the dance finished, one guy walked around on stage with a hand-held microphone. "You all listen up!" he said. "I was once a skinny, scrawny little kid. Didn't get nothing but white bread and hotdogs and macaroni with cheese powder. You hear what I'm saying? All I drank was soda. Any of you dudes eat like that? You hearing me?"

Jonny shrank down against the wall. He hoped the muscled guy with the mic would not notice him.

"Then I started getting sick and depressed all the time," the guy said. His dark eyes seemed to shoot a stare right down the gym and lock onto Jonny's eyes. Jonny held his breath.

"Didn't have any joy in life. Not a single puny muscle. No dancing. You hear me? No sports. I was not eating right! My body needed energy food to grow strong. My body wanted to be a formula one race car, but I wasn't putting any high-grade fuel in it. I was feeding my body junk fuel. I was wrecking my own engines, man!"

Jonny sat up a little straighter. The hyper guy didn't seem to be looking his way anymore.

"I started eating right, I started treating my body right. I gave it protein to build muscles. I gave it fresh food with vitamins. And it got fit!" the man yelled, punching the air. "I started shooting hoops, and pretty soon I was playing like an athlete. I could run! I could jump! I could dance! My body was getting the fuel it needed."

"Look at that guy's abs," Markus whispered across to Jonny in admiration.

Six girls climbed on stage. Their long blonde and brown hair swayed as they walked. They all looked hot and curvy in colored jeans and bright ruffled blouses.

"Nice colors," Brenda whispered. She had shuffled over to where Jonny sat. Now she was eying the girls' clothes.

"Every one of us girls on this stage was once a fat teenager," a tall brunette said into the mic. "We all ate to cope with problems like bullying, depression, traumas, pain. We all thought food was the answer to our problems. But we ate the wrong kind of food and we ate too much of it. So then we just had a bigger problem to deal with. Food didn't solve anything."

Nothing solves anything, Jonny thought miserably.

He didn't think he could relate to muscled guys

or curvy blonde girls. What did they know about his life?

Now another guy walked on stage, a small Asian man.

"Students of Woodside," he said. "I am the manager of this team called Kick It! Every afternoon for the week, my team and I will be in the gym to teach you about making smart choices around food, exercise, and being your personal best. I'm looking forward to getting to know you all!"

"Maybe it'll be more fun than metaphors," Brenda said, nudging Jonny's shoulder.

He shrugged.

But as the week wore on, he decided that Brenda was right. The Kick It! team was full of surprises. They started teaching kids to break dance, to jump skipping ropes, to run up walls, to make healthy snacks like fruit smoothies, to read the labels on food packages. They gave demonstrations of wrestling and judo. They handed out recipes for healthy food. They handed out charts showing how many calories were in different kinds of food, and how much protein, and how much salt, sugar, and fat. On Friday, they gave everyone a list of homework assignments.

"Nobody's gonna check this assignment for you when you've done it," the biggest guy with the mic said. "No teacher's gonna give you a grade on it. This homework is for YOU! You do it, you learn something, you get your problems taken care of for yourself. Hear what I'm saying? You all are in charge of your own lives. Now go and learn some new stuff, and make some smart choices. Feed your bodies formula-one fuel! Give your bodies some exercise. Pretty soon, you'll all be fit. You hearing me?"

"WE'RE HEARING YOU!" hollered the students of Woodside. Jonny surprised himself when his own mouth joined in with a whisper. He folded the homework list and slid it into a pocket.

On the weekend, he flattened it on the island in the kitchen. The first item on the list was to go grocery shopping and read the labelling on the food products.

"Mom, can we do this today?" Jonny asked.

She tossed her hair back and studied the list. "Sure," she agreed. "We'll go to the supermarket while Maria's at a birthday party."

The shopping took Mom and Jonny a whole two hours. They squinted at labels until they were just about in need of glasses.

Jonny had never seen so many long words. Reading labels was worse than reading metaphors. "Disodium phosphate," he said.

"What is all this stuff anyway?" Mom asked.

Jonny consulted another sheet of paper that the Kick It! team had handed out. "It's chemicals put in food to keep it looking fresh even if it's really old,' he said. "Some of the chemicals are to give the food flavor. But the team says that fresh food has enough good flavor of its own. It doesn't need fake flavors added to it. The team says we're supposed to cook using fresh food, not stuff that's already been preserved and put in boxes and cans. Look, assignment two on my list is to make a meal from scratch using only fresh ingredients."

Mom looked doubtful. She blew her bangs off her forehead. "You want to try this today?" she asked.

Jonny shrugged. He thought about his video game, but he was so bored with it. And he thought about shooting hoops with Markus, but it was hard for him to block Markus. He was too heavy and slow.

"Okay, let's cook," he said. "I've got a recipe here. And a list of what we need. The team gave it to everyone."

Cooking was a lot slower and messier than opening take-out boxes. But it was way more interesting. Jonny peeled and stirred, chopped and stirred. Things got thicker and thinner, changed color, went soft or hard. Like in chemistry class, he thought. He imagined that he was a TV chef, leaning over the kitchen island at an imaginary audience, telling them what to do next. A grin tugged at his mouth. Maybe I really could be a chef, he thought.

"First time I've seen your face look like it had a happy thought," Mom said. She ruffled his hair and wiped up a whole lot of mess he'd made on the counter.

By the time Mom and Jonny had a meal ready, Maria was home from the party. Cake crumbs and icing were stuck to her mouth. Jonny wished she'd brought some home for him. She said she wasn't hungry and didn't want anything to eat unless it was pizza. "It's not pizza," Jonny said. "Look, me and Mom have cooked stir fried vegetables with shrimps and curried rice."

Maria stared at it suspiciously. "I'm not hungry," she said.

But when Dad came in the door, he said, "What's that great smell? I'm starving!"

The food tasted pretty excellent. Jonny and Dad both had extra. Then Dad helped to clean up the kitchen.

When the phone rang, it was Brenda. "Mom and I cooked an awesome curry,"

she said. "And then I did my list of calories and stuff. Did you do that yet?"

"I'm doing it now." Jonny pulled his homework assignment out from beneath a stack of clean pans. He started trying to add calorie numbers and lists of fat percentages and sodium percentages while Brenda talked.

"I think you should come back to the animal shelter," she said. "That new dog I'm walking? She's a bit lonely, I think."

"Huh? What new dog?"

"Shade got adopted over Christmas by this, like, nerdy kid who lives across town. He renamed her Spots again!"

"Shade got adopted?"

"Well -- duh. That's why the dogs are at the shelter: to get care until they get new homes."

Jonny's pencil came to a standstill. He stared at the number 42 percent RDA for a few minutes without thinking about it. Instead he was thinking about Shadow's caramel-colored eyes. *Someone else is going* to adopt him? What if they don't treat him right? What if they don't figure out about that tickly place behind his left ear?

"So anyway," Brenda went on, "now I'm walking a little fluffy dog. I can't decide which artist to name her after. But I think Shadow would get along with her. I think you should, like, come back and visit Shadow."

"Yeah," Jonny said slowly. He hadn't been in to see Shadow for weeks. Had Alvin given the dog anything special on Christmas day, like a bone or a toy? Did Shadows miss getting walked? Maybe a new volunteer was already walking him!

Jonny felt awful. Maybe his stomach wasn't used to healthy food. Or maybe he needed something else to eat. Some dessert. A soda.

But that isn't going to solve the problem about Shadow, said a voice in his head. I need to get to the shelter and visit him. ASAP.

"I'll be there tomorrow," he told Brenda. "I've got to finish this cooking thing right now."

He borrowed Dad's calculator to figure out how healthy his meal had been. Then he did a comparison with a pre-packaged meal he found boxed in the freezer. His home-cooked meal rocked! It was way healthier than the ready-made food. It was less fatty, less salty, had more protein, and had more vitamins. It would build muscles. It was formula-one fuel for his body!

In his room, Jonny cracked his closet door open and stared at himself in the mirror. His stomach drooped over his pants. His sweatshirt stretched tight across his chest. It was hard to believe he could change this. But maybe with healthier eating and shooting hoops and skipping rope every day like the team Kick It! had said, he could start changing.

Maybe it isn't too late...maybe I could make it happen. I could get muscles. I could be fit. Anyone can change, and I'm in charge around here. I'm in charge of my life...But how is this going to help with the bullying?

Chapter Eleven

My Enemy is My Friend?

After school the next day, Jonny hurried south to the shelter. Alvin looked up from his desk as Jonny swung the door open.

"Hello, mate," he said in surprise. "Ain't seen you here for a donkey's age. How'd you expect Shadow to lose weight if his personal trainer goes missing in action?"

Jonny shuffled his boots in embarrassment. Snow fell off them onto the mat. What if the shelter didn't want him to come back? Worse yet, what if Shadow was gone?

Alvin ran a hand over his shining bald head. "Relax, kid," he said. "Shadow will be delighted to see you. Right now, he's getting all tidied up."

"The groomer's back?" Jonny asked. He could feel a grin splitting his face wide. Shadow was still here!

"No, the groomer's still sick. Cancer," Alvin said,

tugging gloomily at his ponytail. "But her daughter has come in to do some brushing. Why don't you go back and find them?"

Jonny nodded eagerly, wiped his feet once more, and burst through the swinging doors into the dog cage area. A chorus of yips and barks filled his ears. Noses and brown eyes pressed against the wire.

"Shadow!" Jonny called. The big golden dog was standing on a table and someone was bent over behind him. Jonny glimpsed a brush moving down one of Shadow's shaggy legs.

As Jonny came forward, Shadow's tail began to sweep the air in wide arcs. His mouth grinned. "You remember me, boy!" Jonny exclaimed. A warm feeling rushed through his chest.

Just as he reached to stroke the dog's smooth head, the person holding the brush straightened up. Jonny stared directly into the face of --

Liz?

His hand froze in mid-air.

His whole body froze.

He hardly heard the barking and yipping anymore.

"Wh-what are you doing here?" he asked.

"What does it look like?" Liz said. "I'm brushing dogs."

"But Alvin said – he said that the real groomer has cancer and her daughter was here to brush...oh."

Jonny stared into Liz's narrow face. The dark rings were still under her eyes. Now Jonny knew they were not Goth make-up like they'd been at Halloween. Those dark rings were real. And so was Liz's paleness.

She looks miserable, Jonny realized. Her skinny shoulders were hunched, and her black nail polish was chipped. She'd written the word Mom across the back of one thin hand in different colors of ink.

"Hey, I'm really sorry," Jonny said. "I didn't know about this. I mean, if I'd known -- "

"I don't want to talk about it," Liz said sharply. "I don't want you in my face about it. Right?"

"Right," Jonny said. "Can I help you brush the dogs?"

Liz shrugged. "If you want. My mom's grooming kit is in that bag there. Get a brush and work on Shadow's other side."

Jonny bent to the back pack sitting on the floor. He pulled out a brush with a wooden handle and metal teeth.

"Is this okay?" he asked doubtfully. "This won't hurt Shadow?"

"The teeth all have little round bits on the end so they're not sharp," Liz explained. "Don't press too hard. If you find matted tangles, you might have to cut them out. Shadow's coat is in seriously messed-up condition."

While Jonny and Liz brushed his sides, Shadow's tail kept swinging. He turned his head around sometimes as if to check on what was being done to his coat. His caramel-colored eyes smiled at Jonny. Jonny snipped at tangles with a pair of scissors that Liz slid across the table to him, beneath Shadow's wide belly.

"So why'd you call him Shadow?" Liz asked after awhile.

"No reason," Jonny mumbled, feeling stupid. Then he remembered about Liz's mom and thought he should try harder to be friendly. "Well, it was because of this X-Box game where there's a helper called Shadow. I'm trying to beat the game. But even with my cloak of invisibility, I'm stuck on level six."

"I know that game," Liz said. "My older brother has it. Too bad about the cloak; doesn't work in real life either."

Jonny thought about that for a minute. He brushed the patch of long white hair growing on Shadow's chest.

"What do you mean, doesn't work in real life?" he asked cautiously. Talking to Liz felt like tiptoeing through a mine field.

"Read my lips," Liz snapped. "You're never going to be invisible, so you gotta suck it up and get on with it. That's what my brother tells me when I wish I was invisible. He tells me to stand up to my problems."

"You wish to be invisible...?" Jonny trailed off. Liz always seemed to be drawing attention to herself with her three studs in each ear and her rose tattoo and her high-pitched laugh.

"You're not the only one with problems," Liz said. She stared a challenge at Jonny over Shadow's back. Then she blew a large bubble of pink gum and popped it. The loud snap made the dogs bark.

The doors swung open and the old lady called

Phyllis dashed in, pulled along by five little dogs. Her bright blue glance swept over Liz and Jonny working on Shadow.

"That dog looks ready for the show ring!" she said.

Jonny stood back and admired Shadow. It was true; his golden coat gleamed in soft waves.

"You must have tried out that new shampoo," Phyllis said to Liz.

"Yes, I gave him a good wash," Liz agreed.

"Well you're a great girl to spend your time helping us out here," Phyllis said. For a moment, Liz's face transformed. Jonny stared. Liz's skin glowed pink, her dark eyes sparkled, and her mouth lifted in a smile. Suddenly, he remembered exactly how she'd looked when they were friends, playing on the jungle gym in primary school. She'd had that same kind of sparkle.

"We're nearly finished brushing Shadow now," Liz said.

A horrible thought struck Jonny. "You're not getting Shadow ready – I mean – he hasn't been adopted has he?" Jonny asked.

Phyllis's twinkling blue eyes peered at him between her blue lashes. "I think Shadow's still needed here," she said. "So we'll have to make sure he stays a while longer. I'm waiting for you to walk that weight off him!"

Then she hustled away. Her string of little dogs yapped at all the big dogs in the cages as they ran past. For a few minutes, there was pandemonium.

"How can she make sure Shadow stays?" Jonny asked Liz when the noise died down.

"She's the boss," Liz said with a shrug. "So I guess she can decide whatever she wants."

"I thought she was a volunteer like us!"

"Nope. She owns this place," Liz said, brushing the long fringe on Shadow's tail.

Jonny stared after Phyllis in amazement. He once thought she was old and a bit decrepit, but now he noticed how much energy she had, lugging bags of dog food, rushing around the city with her fists gripping leashes, scrubbing out cages. She's healthy and strong! he thought. And I'm a lot younger than her. So I should be able to reach my goal of being healthy and fit.

"So what did you think about team Kick It?" he asked Liz. He started brushing Shadow's ears; they were sort of clogged up with fur. It was a surprise the dog could hear anything.

Liz shrugged and worked in silence. After a little while she said, "Mom used to make awesome meals. But now she's too sick to eat, you know, from the treatments? So mostly I just eat whatever. Like cold hotdog buns or bags of cheese puffs. My step-dad's supposed to organize trips to buy groceries but he's mostly too busy."

"I'm sorry," Jonny said. All the sparkle had vanished from Liz's face and her mouth was set in a hard line.

"This dog is done. I'm outta here!" she said suddenly. She flung her brush into the bag, and tugged on Shadow's leash. "Down!" she said and the dog jumped to the concrete floor.

"You walking him or you too heavy on your feet for that?" Liz asked spitefully. She tossed the end of the leash at Jonny and he fumbled for it, then slipped one wrist through the loop. For a moment, he felt that familiar shrinking feeling, that feeling he got when people bullied him, and he just wanted to go invisible. Then he squared his shoulders.

"Trash talking me doesn't solve your problems, Liz," he said firmly. "So maybe you should quit it."

A flash of embarrassment crossed Liz's face. She shrugged into a black hoodie,and avoided Jonny's eye as she zipped up her bag of grooming supplies.

"Whatever, see you around," she mumbled, brushing past him and out the door.

Jonny stroked Shadow's smooth forehead. "Come on," he said. "Time for the park."

The park was filled with snow drifts and trails of little kids' boots, dog paws, and big boots. Jonny even saw narrow paw marks with long toes. He thought they were from a racoon that should have been hibernating.

Maybe it got hungry in its nest, Jonny thought. He remembered what the biology teacher had said about animals loading up on calories before they went to sleep for the winter. And I wished I could hibernate like a big grizzly bear. But that would be majorly stupid, really. Cuz then I'd miss cool stuff, like walking Shadow and saving up for a trip to Bermuda and making friends with Markus.

"Hey wait up!" called a voice.

Brenda huffed up behind Jonny, her breath making clouds. She had a fluffy white dog with her.

"Who's this?" Jonny asked as Shadow and the white dog touched noses.

"Alvin calls her Snowball because she's white and fat, but I call her Blanca. It means white in Spanish? It sounds better," Brenda explained. "Alvin says both our dogs need to like majorly lose weight."

Jonny nodded. "We could jog with them," he said.

"Once around the outside path?" Brenda suggested.

They began to jog, fast at first but then more and more slowly. At first the dogs trotted ahead but then they got tired too, panting with their bright pink tongues hanging out. Jonny hoped that Shadow's tongue wasn't going to get frost bitten.

"Got – to – stop -- and rest!" he panted to Brenda. They fell onto a bench that someone had scraped the snow off. The dogs flopped down, pressing their hot bellies onto the snow. Jonny rubbed Shadow's ears. He felt sorry for the dog. He wished Shadow could be as energetic as those dogs on TV that could leap high into the air to catch Frisbees. Shadow was only a young dog. It seemed like he could have so much more fun if he was fitter.

"Do you think these dogs have been eating junk food?" he asked Brenda.

"I'm sure we can get them fit, and us too,"

Brenda said. "Why don't we have a plan to jog them in the park every day?"

Jonny nodded. "I've been thinking about that team Kick It!" he said. "I never saw them at lunch time eating in the school cafeteria."

"Why would they eat there?" Brenda scoffed. "It's all total, you know, junk food. Greasy fries, pizzas that look like they got loaded with salt and then run over on a freeway."

"We're not getting very good meals there," Jonny agreed.

"We should start a petition," Brenda said. "Like, at my old school? Students got a petition going to raise money for safer playground equipment. So we could have a petition for healthier food in the cafeteria."

Jonny thought about this. "I don't know," he said with a sigh. "It sounds like a lot of work. And maybe no one would sign it. Or listen to us. We'd just be asking for trouble."

"Like getting bullied?"

"Yeah."

Jonny got up and began to trudge back along the path. After a moment, Brenda followed him.

"Did you know about Liz's mom?" Jonny asked.

"I found out today. But you know what? Liz is really good with words. Maybe we could get her on our team and she could write the petition. What do you think?'

"I think that sounds seriously crazy. Liz? Are you kidding me? Why would she want to be on our team?

And what team are we on anyway?"

"Well, you know, the team to make a petition," Brenda said. She slapped her red gloves against her purple coat to warm her hands up.

"Forget it," Jonny said.

"You and Liz used to be friends. So you could ask her to do the petition writing."

"I said, forget it!" Jonny walked faster, ignoring Brenda as she panted behind. This was all too complicated and weird. And he was starting to feel that hot-cold panic feeling that thinking about bullies gave him. He was hungry, too. He pawed through all his pockets but he didn't have a snack with him. Dang! He'd already eaten the last of the fruit bars that Mom was buying now.

He almost dragged Shadow up the front steps into the shelter, then into his cage. He made sure that the dog had food and water while Brenda put Blanca away.

"See you!" he called to Brenda as he rushed out.

"Good to know you're back," Alvin said as Jonny passed the front desk. "Gotta get your dog in shape, right?'

"Right!" Jonny mumbled, setting out homewards in the dusk.

In his head, Liz's voice kept saying: You're never going to be invisible, so you gotta suck it up and get on with it.

Chapter Twelve

Eye of The Tiger

I should help Shadow get in shape, Jonny thought as math class droned by. The teacher was scrawling algebra equations on the board, x's and y's.

But if I walk Shadow, Brenda will be there with her stupid petition idea. And Liz might be at the shelter too. Like a spy gathering material about me. Stuff that she and the gang can use to bully me about.

Jonny's stomach griped miserably. The shelter had always seemed like a safe zone for him as well as for the dogs but now it didn't seem so safe. Liz had known all about the shelter before he did; her mom had been grooming dogs there for years.

I won't go, Jonny decided. But then his mind filled with a picture of Shadow's adoring brown eyes and his happily swinging tail. Jonny knew he couldn't let the dog down. As the bell rang to end math class and the school day, Jonny shoved his books into his pack and hurried to the door. He went down the street without looking back, and thankfully, neither Liz nor Brenda caught up to him.

Shadow barked a booming welcome when Jonny reached his cage and snapped on his leash. "Twice around the park today," Jonny said to the dog as they headed south. "No excuses."

They jogged the first lap but then ran out of juice and had to walk the second lap. Maybe they'd get better with practice. Jonny sat on a bench for a breather. He pulled his cell out and thumbed a text to Markus. Hey man, can I join U for rope practice?

Jonny sat for a moment, his thumb hovering over the 'send' button. Twice a week, Markus and the rest of the basketball team stayed behind to use the empty school gym for fitness training. Markus said they bounced balls and shot hoops but also jumped skipping ropes. At first, Jonny thought Markus was joshing around. "Skipping ropes?" he asked with a smirk. "Aren't they only for little girls?"

"They seriously give you a cardio work-out," Markus said. "Lots of top athletes use them in training. I train with a rope at home in the basement."

Jonny's thumb inched closer to the 'send' key on his cell. If he jumped rope with Markus, he'd be able to jog around the park with Shadow maybe three or four times. Really jog, not just huff and puff. He imagined himself and Shadow in a green springtime park, casually and effortlessly speeding past people, weaving around skate boarders and bikers. Shadow would be wolf-lean, wolf-fit. Jonny would have bulging muscles in his legs. It was a great picture.

C'mon, send this text to Markus, said a voice in his head. But still Jonny hesitated. A new picture filled his mind of himself in Markus's basement with a skipping rope. He was bouncing up and down like a rubber ball, one of those super springy ones that flew off everything it hit. All his fat rolls wobbling and flapping as he bounced. His round face jiggling up and down.

"Aaargh!" Shadow looked up and whined when Jonny groaned. He gritted his teeth with determination and plunged his thumb down on the key. After a short time, Markus's reply appeared on the screen. K any time. C U.

Yes! Jonny grinned and rose to his feet. "One more lap," he told Shadow. As they jogged around, Brenda joined them with Blanca and fell into step alongside. They were both panting too much to chat, which was fine and dandy with Jonny. The less talk the better.

Afterwards, Jonny took Shadow back and then headed across the street to a pizza place. "Two slices of all-dressed," he said, digging in his pocket for change.

Dad had given him lunch money, but Jonny had skipped lunch. He kept thinking about what Brenda said about greasy fries and salt-loaded pizza. If he wanted to get fit, he had to eat better than that. But the problem with skipping lunch was that he was ravenous after school. So ravenous his hunger attacked his willpower with Ninja speed and strength. His willpower was helpless against these savage attacks. The hunger took no prisoners.

Now, as Jonny waited for his slices of hot pizza, his mouth filled with drool. He glanced around and wiped his chin. He wasn't actually slobbering, was he? How gross would that be?

Nope, his chin was dry. He reached out and took the bag with the pizza, then bolted out the door. Fumbling because of his gloves and his hunger, he crammed a slice into his mouth and bit down. A sigh of relief seemed to pass right through his entire body. But guilt followed as he munched through both slices at rapid speed. He'd refused to eat pizza at lunch, but what was the point, because now he was eating it anyway?

Maybe I really should ask Liz to help with a petition, he thought. If I could eat better at lunch, I wouldn't be so crazy with hunger after school, and I wouldn't be spending my lunch money on fast food. I'd better head to Markus's house.

Jonny texted Mom to let her know where he was going, then turned left at the next intersection. Markus lived in a sprawling ranch house with junipers clipped into strange spiral shapes. Jonny thought they looked like they'd been tortured but maybe they were expensive and fancy.

Markus answered the door when the bell chimed. "Hey, Jonny." He swung the door wide and Jonny stepped in, kicking his boots off and then straightening them on the mat. "I'm just starting my reps," Markus said. "Come on."

Their feet thudded down the carpeted basement stairs into a room lit with florescent strips. Techno music was playing.

"Cool! You like this band?" Jonny asked. "I have their new release. I can lend you the CD."

"Great," Markus agreed.

The metal arms and wires and bars of an exercise machine loomed in one corner. Jonny glanced at it in envy and dismay. Did Markus know how to operate it? It looked like a piece of robotic innards. Weights were stacked nearby. Jonny gripped one of his own slack biceps and hoped Markus wouldn't notice.

"So ropes, right?" Markus said. He tossed one towards Jonny and then positioned himself on the blue rubber matting. Suddenly, Markus's rope became a blur of speed. It whipped against the floor. It whistled through the air. Markus's toes seemed to barely clear the rope as he jumped, moving so fast that he was a blur too.

Jonny gulped. He positioned himself alongside Markus and flung his rope over his head. He wasn't sure how to make it whirl so fast. He hopped, too late. Just like those ropes on the gym climbing wall, the skipping rope tangled around his podgy ankles. Hog-tied, gloated Steve's voice in his head. Face flaming, Jonny bent to untangle himself, waiting for Markus to snicker. But Markus was too busy counting his own jumps out loud. Besides, Markus didn't snicker at other people's misfortunes. He was mostly very matter-of-fact about everything. He was a totally okay guy, and Jonny felt lucky to have him as a buddy.

Jonny flung the rope into the air again and jumped. This time, he cleared the rope. He swung it faster, jumped faster. "...two, three, four," he counted as he jumped. He stepped on the rope and jerked himself to a halt. He tried again. "...eight, nine, ten..."

His ribs heaved. Black dots swung in front of his eyes. His arms ached.

Markus wasn't kidding when he said this was a cardio work-out!

Markus reached two hundred – Jonny could hear him counting – and then walked over to a bench along the wall. He sat down for a rest and gulped from a bottle of water. Distracted, Jonny lost count of how many times he'd jumped his own rope. He needed a drink and a rest too.

"Wanna play a few levels of something?" Markus asked.

Jonny glanced at his watch. "I need to head home for dinner. Catch you next time. Thanks, man."

"No problem, any time," Markus said. He raised his hand and gave Jonny a high five, and then went with Jonny to the front door. Something in the house smelled delicious, meaty and rich. Jonny hoped that Mom was cooking something that smelled as good.

He was in luck. When he reached home, Mom was making Irish stew with Maria's help. This meant that Maria was mostly just eating raw carrots and celery that should have gone into the stew.

"Does this take long to cook?" Jonny asked anxiously.

Mom laughed. "Have a carrot stick and go do your homework," she said. "Dinner is in an hour."

"But Mom, I'm starving!"

"Honey, don't exaggerate," Mom said and turned her back as she opened the fridge.

For a minute, Jonny missed those days when she always had soda and donuts waiting for him after school. But this new, healthy-foods-only trip that she was on was his own fault. He was the one who'd told her that he wanted to feed his body formula-one fuel. He was the one who'd given her all the sheets of information and recipes from team Kick It! So he couldn't be mad at Mom now. And besides, he was supposed to be setting an example to Maria; Mom and Dad were worried about how plump she was growing.

Last week, at school, some losers had told his little sister they weren't going to play with her anymore. This was after Maria got stuck on the jungle gym. "They called me a fatso," Maria had told everyone at the dinner table. Johnny had felt enraged. Mom and Dad had flashed each other eye-signals, and later Dad had stuck his head in the door of Johnny's room. "Hey, son," Dad said, "try and just eat what your mom buys now without complaining? We want you to help us with Maria's weight."

What am I – a fitness expert? Jonny had thought. But then later, he thought that maybe he was, in his own way. He'd done all the homework assignments from team Kick It! He'd learned how to read food labels and how to make healthy snacks, and he was working on getting Shadow and himself slimmer. I really am taking charge of my own life, he'd realized. This felt good; better than the good feeling of beating a level, or of eating a bag of popcorn. This was the kind of good that felt like it might stick around, last for a long while.

Tonight, in his room, Jonny did his homework while he waited for the stew to cook. The smell of it curled under his door and tickled his nostrils. If only the cafeteria at school smelled as good instead of smelling like floor wash and old grease and stale crusts.

Maybe I should talk to Liz, Jonny thought. But then Steve might leap in with both feet. And kick the daylights out of me. Is it worth the risk?

Chapter Thirteen

GOOOALS!

Finding a safe time and place to talk to Liz without getting hassled by Steve and Pete was hard. First, Jonny tried in the cafeteria line but just as he shuffled up behind Liz, Steve walked through the door. Jonny caved and moved quickly away from Liz. He tried again near the lockers but then realized that Pete was standing only two feet away. Pete's freckled face and sandy hair were half-hidden by his open locker door. Jonny caved again, fumbling with his locker combination, sweat breaking out on his forehead. Then he tried to talk to Liz after English class. She had stayed behind to gab to Ms. Singh about something. Jonny waited outside the door.

Finally Liz came out and began sauntering down the hall. Jonny sucked in a deep breath and followed her.

"Hey, um, Liz," he said. She glanced over her

shoulder but kept walking.

"I wasn't gonna hurt her," she said suddenly.

"Wh-what?" Jonny blinked in surprise.

"Your sister at Halloween," Liz said. "I just wanted to give her a swing ride."

"No problem," Jonny said. He darted a glance up and down the hall. He might not have much time, and he needed to explain about the petition. He walked faster until he was alongside Liz.

"I was like wondering if you'd help me - well, Brenda and me - with something?"

"Depends," Liz said with a shrug.

"We were thinking of getting a petition going about the cafeteria food--"

Jonny's words trailed into silence as Steve suddenly strode from the guy's washroom. He stomped over and leaned threateningly towards Jonny. Jonny took a step back. Dang. Why was it so hard to hold his ground with Steve?

"Is Jelly Fatso bothering you?" Steve asked Liz.

For once, Liz ignored Steve.

"I was telling her about a petition," Jonny said.

Steve sneered. "The only petition Liz is going to sign is a petition asking Woodside Jr. High to get rid of YOU," he said. He flexed his arm under Jonny's nose. Jonny took another step back.

"See these muscles?" Steve asked. "See this fist?" He clenched his knuckles and swung his fist hard and fast. It whistled under Jonny's chin. "This fist is waiting for you after school. It wants to give you a lesson you won't forget. Now beat it!"

Steve stepped right up to Jonny, his broad chest almost shoving Jonny off his feet. Jonny grabbed at his backpack strap as it slipped on his shoulder. Then he turned and rushed along the hall. His heart hammered with fear and something else. Anger. That's what it was. He was sick and tired of letting Steve be the boss of him. But he couldn't figure out what to do about it.

It was the last period of the day now, and Jonny had a spare. He went to the library and slumped at a desk in a quiet corner. For a while, he just stared into space and waited for his heart rate to slow down. Man, if his body and his brain could move as fast as his heart, he'd be Superman. Finally, after he'd calmed down, he pulled his homework out. If he got it done now, then he'd have more time at the shelter after school.

If I can make it to the shelter without meeting Steve's fists, he thought.

He stared at his English homework assignment. Ms. Singh was on a roll about everyone setting themselves goals for English class. They were all supposed to identify their areas of weakness and set themselves goals to work on, like improving their spelling or learning how to use apostrophes properly or getting better at essay format.

"Part of learning is figuring out what you need to learn. You need to take responsibility for your own learning," Ms. Singh had said. Jonny thought that was sort of the same as being in charge of your own life.

My Goals, Jonny wrote. Then he chewed on his

pen for a bit. His brain didn't seem to want to concentrate on paragraphs or punctuation. It was running around like a hamster in a wheel, trapped inside one thought. That thought was how scary Steve was.

Jonny gave his head a shake.

1. Survive school, he wrote.
2. That's the only goal I have? he wondered. What a loser goal. What else?
3. Lose weight so I can snorkel in the Bahamas!! If we even go.
4. Beat the final level.
5. Talk to Liz no matter what and do a petition to eat better at school.
6. Ask Mom and Dad if I can adopt Shadow if I lose 15 pounds by Spring Break. If I could even do this.
7. Learn how to cook. Be a chef (???)
8. Remember that I'm in charge of my life!!!

Reading his list through, Jonny felt a surge of energy. All that adrenalin his heart pumped around must have got his brain into high gear. Or maybe it was because he was feeding his brain formula-one fuel now so it was performing fast and smooth for him. This was a great list! Jonny read it through once more, grinning.

Before the bell rang for end of school, he pounded down the empty hall to Liz's locker. Quickly, before anyone else arrived there, he taped a little piece of paper to the door. On it, he'd written just one word: Shadow. Liz would know what it meant but no one else would. Jonny flung his coat over one arm and vamoosed outside, reaching the front steps just as the bell rang. He took the steps two at a time, circled the buses, and began to jog south to the shelter before Steve could even get out the front door of school.

Phyllis was at the desk today instead of Alvin, clicking away at the computer keyboard. She sent Jonny a pointy smile as he came in.

"Hey, um, hi!" Jonny said. "Can I talk to you about Shadow?"

"Talk away," said Phyllis.

"I'm trying to lose weight, so Shadow and I are jogging around the park every night. And I thought maybe I could ask my parents if I could have Shadow if I can lose fifteen pounds by spring break. Like, they might let me have him as a reward. It's on my goal list that I made this afternoon. But only if you can keep Shadow here at the shelter until then and not let him get adopted by anyone else?"

Jonny stopped to take a breath. His words had come charging out of his mouth at top speed.

Phyllis's eyes twinkled at him. "I will personally make sure that Shadow does not go to any other home," she said. "Now go and get his leash."

"Oh wow! I mean, wow—thank you!"

Jonny got Shadow from his cage and asked him to jump onto the grooming table. He started working on some tangles in the dog's coat with the comb he kept in his own back pocket. He was pretty sure, when he heard the front door open, that Liz was arriving.

Yes! She sauntered in, looking a bit scared but determined.

"What's this mean?" she asked, waving Jonny's note.

"I wanted you to come to the shelter so I could talk to you. Without Steve bothering us," Jonny said.

"Steve doesn't bother me," Liz said. She shot a glare at Jonny and popped her gum.

"Brenda and I want to do a petition so that the school cafeteria serves better lunches. Not all that stale, greasy stuff. Salads and fruit and fresh stuff instead. You know, like team Kick It! said."

"Yeah, so what?" Liz asked.

"You're good with words," Jonny said. "Could you write the petition for us? And then Brenda and I can take it around and get it signed."

Liz blew another bubble and snapped it. The dogs all barked. "I guess," she agreed. "I'm kinda bummed about living on junk."

"That's awesome!" Jonny said.

The door swung open again, and the dogs all jumped up. Brenda came in, her cheeks rosy with cold, her nose glowing. She stopped when she saw Liz, and her face tightened with anxiety.

"It's okay," Jonny said. "Liz is going to help us with the petition."

Brenda's round face relaxed into her wide, open smile. Jonny stared at her for a moment. Brenda might have a chubby chin but she also had a truly radiant smile.

"I was thinking we could put the petition online," Brenda said. "I could ask the principal if it could go to all the students' and parents' emails. I was thinking I could make posters for the school hallways too. You know, my mom could help me design them and make them bright and colorful."

"I'm sure they'd be bright," Liz said sarcastically. Then she bit her lip and flushed. "Sorry," she mumbled.

There was an awkward silence. Shadow swung his tail, thumping it against Jonny.

"Posters would be cool; you're good at art and designing stuff," Jonny told Brenda.

"And Pete is good at computers," said Brenda. "Maybe we could ask Pete to help with getting the posters scanned. He could put them on Woodside's web site. He's the student web master."

Pete? Jonny's heart sank. He didn't want to work with Pete, with his sticking out ears and his bean-pole body. He hated the way Pete always tagged along in Steve's shadow, like he couldn't wait to do whatever Steve told him to.

But it's true, Pete's a geek as well as a cheat, Jonny thought. So maybe Brenda is right. Maybe we need Pete to help with this. And maybe if we get Pete to help us, he'll stop being such a pain in the neck and bullying us...?

"Hey, Liz," Jonny said. "Can you ask Pete to work on this?"

"Nope," Liz said. "It's your petition."

"No, it's a petition for all Woodside students,

including you," said Jonny firmly.

"I'm already writing the words," Liz snapped. "So you ask Pete yourself."

Jonny sighed. He glanced at Brenda but her face had that scared look again. He couldn't ask her to talk to Pete. He'd have to ask Pete himself. But how?

Shadow whined impatiently, and Jonny gave the dog a head rub. "Park time," he said, and Shadow jumped eagerly from the table.

"Wait for me and Blanca," Brenda said.

"Are you coming, Liz?" Jonny asked but she shook her head.

"I'm going to groom Patches," she said.

"Can we work on the petition this weekend...like texting about it?" Jonny asked.

"I guess." Liz turned away to the cages and let out a brown and white hound.

After jogging in the park with Brenda, Jonny went over to Markus's and jumped rope to one hundred. He even did a few bench presses. Then he hitched up his pants – they were getting loose around the waist – and hurried home. It was Friday night and this meant that Dad came home early. He and Jonny had a deal going for Friday nights. Jonny would choose a recipe from a web site of healthy foods that he'd done a Google search for. He'd text Dad a list of ingredients, and Dad would buy them on the way home from work. Then he and Jonny would cook a gourmet meal for Maria and Mom. On her way home from work, Mom would stop by the movie store and rent something they could all watch together after dinner.

Tonight though, after dinner, Jonny needed to talk to his parents. He kept trying out different opening lines in his head, lines like Oh hey, that dog I told you about? or I know you said I couldn't have a dog but...or You guys should come to the shelter and meet Shadow...

The important thing, he decided, was to keep his tone super casual. Stay cool. Like the topic didn't really matter.

But just as Dad started gathering plates from the table, Jonny's mouth opened. Words blurted out like stampeding cattle. Urgent, wild words.

"You said I couldn't have a dog," he said. "But there's this dog at the shelter. He really likes me and -- "

Dad set the plates down. His brow furrowed. Mom sent him a flashing glance.

Jonny's words plunged on. "Ms. Singh, my English teacher, she said to set goals. And my list of goals is to lose fifteen pounds by spring break. And then I thought maybe you'd let me have Shadow as a reward. He's a good dog! No problems! And now that Mom isn't working so late, we have more time for a dog. And I'm walking him in the park every night, anyway. Well, jogging. Shadow needs to lose weight too."

His words stopped just as suddenly as they'd started.

There was a long silence at the table.

"I want Shadow to live here!" Maria suddenly piped up. Mom tossed her hair back and smiled at Dad.

Dad's brow softened.

"Jonny, you're trying real hard with this fitness goal," he said. "A good effort deserves a reward. So if you can lose that weight, you can have Shadow. But not until after spring break, because for break we're going on vacation."

"We are?"

"Your mom bought the tickets to Bermuda today."

"YES! Woo-hoo! YES! " Jonny couldn't' believe his luck! He jumped up, laughing, then kissed Mom and gave Maria a squeeze. Dad got him in a headlock, and they wrestled around the kitchen while Dad rubbed his knuckles into Jonny's hair.

"Time to get these dishes washed," Dad said at last, and Jonny started running hot water for the pans.

Washing up, he thought, Now, if I can just get through the next few weeks at school...

Chapter Fourteen

The Jedi Mind Trick

Over the weekend, Jonny hung out with Markus and told him about the petition for better food at school. Markus promised to get the guys on the basketball team to sign it. Liz texted to say that she was working on the wording of the petition, and Brenda texted to say that she was painting bright posters for the school walls. R U asking Pete about it? she wrote. Jonny sighed. ???? he texted back.

On Monday, Liz showed them what she'd written.

We, the undersigned students of Woodside Jr. High School, and the adults associated with the Woodside community, petition the school board to reconsider the serving of fast food in its cafeteria. The students of Woodside deserve healthy fresh food, with vitamins and minerals, and a balance of carbohydrates and protein. The current meals do not meet these nutritional requirements. We are tired of the cafeteria's greasy, salt,y and unhealthy foods.

"Wow, good wording," Jonny said when he read it.

"My mom helped me a bit," Liz said. For a moment, her face sparkled. "She's doing better now she's finished her treatments."

Brenda patted Liz's shoulders. "That's awesome," she said, and Jonny repeated, "Yeah, awesome."

"Now we need to meet with the principal," Brenda said.

Later, in the office of Mr. Brecker, the principal, they explained their idea. Mr. Brecker agreed to send the petition out to parents and students using the school's address book of emails. He also agreed they could ask students to sign-up on hard copies in the hallways between classes. Brenda asked if her posters could be hung on bulletin boards in classrooms and hallways, and Mr. Brecker agreed to this too.

"We could even put a scan of one of your posters on Woodside's web site," he offered. Liz and Brenda both stared at Jonny. He flushed and shuffled his feet.

"Well, I'm...um...I'm working on that," he said.

But the only place he was working on it was inside his own head because he still hadn't decided to ask Pete. Or how to ask Pete. Or when to ask Pete. He still flinched when he remembered Steve's fist whistling past his chin a week ago and sinking into his guts at Halloween. He didn't want another swollen sore eye;

one had been bad enough. What was he supposed to do? Be a one-eyed cripple for life just because of some petition? You could be a coward for life instead, nagged a voice in his head.

The two words kept tumbling around in his brain like lottery balls in a basket. Coward. Cripple. Coward. Cripple.

By the end of school on Wednesday, Jonny couldn't take it any more. He knew he had to stand up for himself. Liz and Brenda were circulating in the crowd of students waiting for the buses, getting signatures on the petition. They even boarded the buses and got the drivers to sign.

Jonny leaned against a wall, trying to blend, trying to look cool. He tensed as Steve and Pete strolled past, yammering on about some music download they were pirating. Jonny waited until they were half-way across the white field, trudging along the path that students had worn in the snow. Then he jogged after them.

"Yo, I've got something to say to you!" he called out.

Steve and Pete swung around. A flicker of surprise crossed Steve's face, then he scowled meanly.

"Jelly Fatso," he said. "Come to kiss my fists again?"

"I'm here to talk to Pete," Jonny said bravely, holding his ground. He was totally determined not to take even one tiny step backwards, away from Steve.

Pete looked shocked, his freckled face frozen as if

he didn't know what to do or say. He glanced at Steve for orders.

"Pete, you're the student web master for the school," Jonny said. "We need your help with the healthy food petition."

Steve shoved Pete aside and stepped towards Jonny.

"Hey!" Steve snarled. He shoved his face into Jonny's. Jonny felt himself flinch but he willed his legs not to move, to be like rods of steel holding up a tall building. His legs would not bend or sway. He glared back into Steve's eyes.

"I'm not talking to you," he said quietly. "I'm talking to Pete."

"Oh yes, you are talking to me. And I'm a lean mean fightin' machine. You're way out of your league, Fatso."

And that was when it happened. Right then, when Jonny was glaring into Steve's face and willing his legs not to run away with him. That was when Jonny had his totally epic and brilliant idea.

"Well, yeah," he agreed with Steve. "I do need to talk to you too. I'm hoping you can help with the petition."

"As if," Steve guffawed and Pete, standing behind him, snickered too.

"I mean it," Jonny said. "I need you to write a rap, like your Halloween rap. Only you need to use the words lean BUT NOT mean. Then you can sing the rap at assembly on Friday. Brenda and I are giving a presentation at assembly about the petition. You can be part of it."

"As if," Steve repeated. But his voice was quieter. He took one step back. "Why would I want to be part of your lame idea?"

"Because you need to eat healthy food to build muscles for boxing," said Jonny. "You need healthy lunches more than any of us."

Steve was silent, kicking at snow. Jonny was almost sure he was going to cave. He knew that Steve liked to rap and be on stage. He also liked to brag about his boxing muscles. How could he resist Jonny's idea?

"And Pete, you can help by scanning one of Brenda's posters about healthy eating and about the petition. We need it uploaded onto Woodside's web site."

Pete's ears glowed pink. He shrugged and glanced nervously at Steve.

"We'll think about it," Steve said. "Now get lost, Fatso."

He and Pete turned and trudged away through the snow. Jonny wanted to give a victory whoop but he figured that might be pushing his luck. Instead he whispered "Yes!" to himself and jogged back to tell the girls.

In computer lab next day, Pete asked Brenda for a poster and scanned it. Then he uploaded it onto the web site with a heading about how students were trying to get the school board to arrange healthier lunches in the cafeteria.

Jonny didn't know yet whether Steve was writing a rap. He was a little scared to go and ask him; he figured ignorance was bliss, as the saying went. But by Friday morning, he knew he'd have to track Steve down early, before assembly, and find out what was happening. He jogged down the road as the sun rose. Purple and pink shadows lay over the snow. Garbage cans lined the curb, waiting for the collection truck.

In the school yard, Jonny saw Steve and Pete huddled by the dumpster. Liz wasn't with them. Jonny suddenly realized that Liz hadn't been hanging out with the gang all week. She'd been too busy circulating the petition. So Steve doesn't really have a gang anymore, Jonny thought. Pete doesn't make a gang all by himself.

This thought made him cheerful. He grinned as he strode over to the two boys.

"Got your rap ready?" he called to Steve.

Steve tapped his forehead. "It's all in here," he said.

"So you're on after Mr. Brecker," Jonny said.

Steve gave a mocking salute and turned away. Jonny grinned again and jogged towards the buses to find Liz and Brenda.

Assembly in the gym began with Mr. Brecker sharing school news with students. Today he talked about the petition being circulated to ask the school board for a healthier lunch menu in the Woodside cafeteria. Liz went onstage, looking good in a new purple sweater and black jeans. She explained to students how team Kick It! had given them the idea of having healthier food at lunch. "We need to be offered formula-one food," Liz said. "Not fatty, greasy stuff. We need pure fruit juice or water instead of soda. We need brain food. Woodside students are gonna rock!"

"Rah, rah, Woodside rocks!" everyone in the gym yelled.

Then Steve sauntered on stage, looking nonchalant, flexing his biceps. Pete scuttled after him and turned on the music. Students sitting on the floor swayed to the beat. Pete and Liz danced; Jonny had to admit that they had some funky moves.

Steve grabbed the hand-held mic and began to sing.

I'm lean, yo! I'm a fit machine,
My brain's runnin' clean.
Us Woodside students we're gonna be cool,
In the cafeteria us rude dawgs rule.
We ain't gonna eat no junk food,
Punk food, fast food.
I'm lean, you're lean,
We're lean machines
Runnin' on clean,
We're runnin' good,
We're on formula-one food.
Yo, you all hearin' me?
We're lean but we AIN'T mean!

Pete did a somersault and Liz did the splits. Steve stared over the mic straight at Jonny and gave another mocking salute. Jonny felt his face glow with amazement. This was my own idea – and it worked. I really can change things in my own life!

All around Jonny, the students went wild, roaring and clapping. Mr. Brecker took the mic back and waited for silence. "Students," he said. "Students of Woodside!" Gradually the noise died down.

"I'd like the members of team Lean But Not Mean to stop by my office now. Our local FXL television station would like to interview them. The rest of you are dismissed for class."

Television? Interview? What -- ?

Jonny's jaw hung open in shock.

Chapter Fifteen

My Victory

Mr. Brecker's office was not a place Jonny had spent much time before, although he figured that Steve probably felt right at home in there. Today after assembly, the office was crowded. There was Mr. Brecker sitting behind his desk with its photos of his children, a pink plastic sausage dog (what was that about? Jonny wondered), and a stack of files.

Then there was the TV camera man: a short pudgy guy with earrings and a big piece of black equipment resting on his shoulder. He swivelled from the hips, turning the camera's lens around like a big eye. When the eye focused on his own face, Jonny fidgeted with nerves.

Besides the pudgy camera man was a skinny dude who didn't look old enough to be working for TV but he seemed to be the reporter. He was the one who asked all the questions.

Finally, there were Steve, Pete, Liz, Brenda, and Jonny standing along the wall.

"So kids," the skinny dude said, "talk to me about this petition."

His big furry microphone looked like a caterpillar having a bad hair day; maybe even a caterpillar that had stuck its nose into an electrical outlet. He held it into the middle of the room. There was an awkward silence.

The skinny dude lifted an eyebrow at Jonny. "Who had the idea and why?" he asked.

Jonny licked his lips and tried to stare straight into the camera without flinching. "It was really Brenda's idea," he said. "After team Kick It! visited our school."

"Who's Brenda?" the guy asked.

Brenda raised one hand and flushed pink; she bestowed her awesome smile on the camera. Suddenly Jonny felt himself relax. This is going to give our idea perfect publicity, he thought. The school board will have to cave after this airs on the evening news!

"It was really Jonny who got us all working together," Brenda said. Then she explained about team Kick It! and feeding your body formula-one fuel and exercising to build muscle and to get fit. She talked about how Steve rapped and Liz wrote the petition and Pete did the web site.

"And we're getting exercise with shelter dogs," Jonny added. He explained about Shade and Blanca and Shadow and Patches. He even explained how he was going to get Shadow as a reward for losing fifteen pounds.

"Think you can make this goal?" the reporter asked. For just a moment, a flicker of doubt ran through Jonny. Then he remembered that he was in control of his life. He straightened his shoulders. "I KNOW I can do it!" he said, and he grinned confidently.

Then the skinny reporter talked to the other kids -- to the gang, Jonny thought as Steve talked about building up muscles for boxing and how he wanted to box in the Olympics. I can't believe I'm working on the same project as the gang, Jonny thought. Only I don't think they really are a gang, not anymore.

"And how many signatures do you have now?" the reporter asked.

"Five hundred and twelve," said Liz proudly.

"Who is going to present them to the school board?"

"I am taking them myself," said Mr. Brecker, rising from behind his desk. "I will present them at the next meeting of the board and committee members on Tuesday evening next week."

"FXL Television wishes you all the best of luck with this fab-u-lous project to make fitness and healthy eating part of your lives!" said the reporter. The camera man turned his equipment off and shook hands with everyone. "Great work, man," he said when he shook hands with Jonny. "Hope everything works out for you."

After this excitement, the rest of the week dragged past as slowly as a sleep-deprived snail. In

English class, Jonny handed in the wrong set of goals. Ms. Singh read in silence about surviving school, losing weight, and being in charge of one's own life. The she peered at Jonny over her glasses. For a moment, Jonny thought he was going to get a lecture. But then Ms. Singh smiled and said, "Super goals, although you won't be able to complete them in my class...and your punctuation is rather excitable. Make a new goal sheet for this class, Mr. Fatzio. At the top of it write: I need to learn to use correct punctuation."

"Sure thing," Jonny said while Brenda and Liz giggled.

In math class, the teacher decided to talk about ratios, and they had to figure out what ratio of the students had signed the petition and what ratio of the citizens of Woodside had signed it. In chemistry, they played around with food coloring, and the rising powers of yeast and baking powder.

Finally, the week ended, and the weekend rolled by without much exciting happening – except for Woodside Junior High's TV segment airing. Jonny's family crowded onto the couch to watch it. Jonny's hands were sweating with nerves but then he started grinning. They all looked and sounded okay! Brenda's tee, aqua with pink swirls, brightened up Mr. Brecker's beige office. Liz's ear studs – all six of them – sparkled and Liz's smile sparkled too. Pete's ears glowed. Steve looked so serious when he talked about boxing for the Olympics that Jonny really hoped this would happen one day.

Then I can say I once got punched out by someone famous, he joked to himself.

After Jonny talked on-screen about losing weight to earn Shadow, Dad chuckled. "Now you've announced it to the whole world on TV, I guess your mom and I can't back out on the deal," he said.

"Nope, he's got us out-smarted!" Mom agreed with a laugh.

Jonny didn't mind them teasing. He'd seen the bag of dog food sitting in the garage and the plastic bowls that his parents had already bought.

Finally it was Tuesday – the evening for Principal Brecker to take the petition to the school board meeting. Jonny tried not to think about it as he did his homework. Brenda called and asked, "When will we know what's going on?"

"Tomorrow?" Jonny asked. "Hope they decide quick!"

In the morning, a special assembly was called and Principal Brecker went on stage with the mic. "Team Lean But Not Mean, I need you up here," he said. Jonny and Brenda glanced at each other. Brenda looked as nervous and shocked as Jonny felt. In fact, his stomach seemed to be break dancing and his legs seemed to have gone sort of numb. He wasn't sure they could carry him up there...on the stage? In front of everyone? To be snickered at?

"Get going man." Markus stuck an elbow in Jonny's ribs. He lumbered to his feet; for a moment, he felt like a buffalo again, a hippo, a whale. He stumbled through the rows of students seated on the gym floor. He tripped up the steps onto the stage and stared out over the sea of faces. All those eyes, looking right at – him with his bulging belly and his flabby muscles!

After a minute, Jonny's vision cleared. He realised that no one in the crowd was snickering. He straightened up, remembering that he'd already lost weight and was already developing muscles from jumping ropes and jogging in the park. He hitched up his pants and stood taller.

What was Mr. Brecker talking about? Jonny zoned in and realised that the Principal was praising them for their great effort and great team work.

"Last night," he said, "the committee and board members unanimously passed a decision to find a new catering company for your school. It is going to give the contract to a catering company that can provide fresh, healthy meals at lunch so that you can all give your bodies formula-one fuel. And give your brains formula-one fuel. I'll be expecting great grades from everyone. Go, Woodside!"

"Rah, rah, Woodside!" yelled all the students.

"Go, team Lean But Not Mean!" yelled Mr. Brecker, waving the microphone.

"Rah rah, Lean But Not Mean!" yelled the students.

They whistled and cheered and drummed their heels on the floor, and someone tossed a hat into the air and it got stuck on an open window.

Jonny felt a surge of energy and amazement. He

wasn't going to be Jelly Fatso around here anymore. He was going to be one of those team guys who helped get Woodside school on TV and bring better food to the cafeteria! It all felt like a dream but it wasn't a dream or a video game – it was real.

"We hope the new catering company can take over the cafeteria after spring break," Mr. Brecker said. "Assembly dismissed."

After this, no one jostled Jonny into locker doors or tied together the laces of his sneakers or hit him in the back of the neck with snowballs. People gave him high-fives in the hallways and asked for his help with their chemistry homework. When a player left the basketball team, Markus told Jonny he should try out for it. "You could play great defense," he said.

"You really think so?" Jonny asked.

"Totally. Your cardio's up for it...you can jump rope as good as me now!"

Steve stopped bullying Jonny. He didn't exactly turn into a buddy -- he just mostly ignored Jonny, although once in a while, catching Jonny's eye, he'd give him that mocking salute. Pete moved away to go to a different school with a better computer lab. Liz and Brenda teamed up to make a special section in the Year Book; Liz was writing poems about school happenings, and Brenda was creating pictures to go with the poems.

When school let out for spring break, Jonny jogged south towards the shelter. Melting snow splashed against his legs. His sneakers slapped the wet pavement with a strong, steady rhythm, and his lungs filled up deep with misty air. An early robin hopped on the brown grass, searching for worms.

"You're going north, I'm going south," Jonny muttered as he jogged past the bird. Woo-hoo, I'm going south to snorkel with reef fish. Maybe even rays or sharks! Now my cardio's so great, I can dive deeper and stay down longer! This holiday is gonna rock big time!

Jonny bounded up the shelter steps two at a time.

"Whoa there, someone's in a good mood!" Alvin said, winding a band around his ponytail. Jonny grinned. "I'm just saying goodbye to Shadow," he said. "Then we're heading to the airport."

"Can't keep the pilot waiting," Alvin said. "Get going!"

Jonny swung through the doors and the dogs barked and yapped in their cages. Phyllis had Shadow up on the grooming table, running a comb through his shaggy leg hair. When Shadow saw Jonny, he let out an excited bark and grinned, showing his white teeth and pink lip frills. His tail whacked Phyllis on the shoulder.

"Someone's happy to see you!" Phyllis said, the light shining on her big round glasses.

Jonny flung his arms around the big dog's neck and hugged him. Shadow slobbered his tongue against Jonny's face.

"So, how that's weight loss coming along?" Phyllis asked.

"I think he's lost more," Jonny said. "Don't you think he's looking better? I'm going to buy him a new Frisbee. Do you think he could learn to jump for it?"

Phyllis laughed. "I'm sure he could," she said. "But I was talking about your own weight loss."

"Oh! I've lost twelve pounds out of that fifteen – just three more to go."

"Think you can do it?"

"I know I can...all that swimming I'm gonna do, all that fresh fish and pineapple I'll eat. I can totally lose three pounds on this trip to Bermuda. When I get back, I'll come to take Shadow home."

"You're the man!" said Phyllis, and she handed the dog's leash to Jonny.

The End

Jonny's Tropical Smoothie

Ingredients:
1 orange
½ Cup pineapple (fresh or canned)
Half a banana
2/3 Cup orange juice
Two drops of vanilla essence
2 tablespoons of yoghurt (plain, vanilla or citrus flavor work best)
½ Cup of ice cubes

Caution:
To make this delicious and nutritious breakfast or snack, you will need a food blender. Make sure to have an adult help you operate the blender safely. Never stick your fingers inside, or the sharp blades will cut you. Never operate an electric appliance with damp or wet hands.

How to make:

1. Peel the orange and chop it into cubes.

2. Open the can of pineapple, if you are using canned fruit. If you are using fresh pineapple, cut the outside layers off, cut the fruit into slices, and then cut the slices into cubes.

3. Peel the banana and cut half of it into cubes.

4. Add the ice to the blender. On the 'chop' setting, blend the ice until it is in small pieces.

5. Add the juice to the blender. On the 'liquefy' setting, blend until the contents of the blender are slushy.

6. Add the fruit, yoghurt, and vanilla flavoring.

7. Blend everything on the 'liquefy' setting until smooth (about one minute).

Pour into a tall glass and enjoy!

You can experiment to make special smoothies of your own – you can use frozen fruit instead of ice, or ice-cream instead of yoghurt, or milk instead of juice. You can add any kind of fruit that you like! Smoothies are quick to make and nutritious to drink, packed full of vitamins and minerals.